Follow That Mom!

Follow That Mom!

Mary Riskind

Houghton Mifflin Company
Boston 1986

Library of Congress Cataloging-in-Publication Data

Riskind, Mary.
  Follow that mom!

  Summary: Eleven-year-old Maxine creates as much
mischief as possible in order to convince her mother
to quit the Girl Scouts.
  [1. Mothers and daughters—Fiction. 2. Girl Scouts—
Fiction] I. Title.
PZ7.R493Fo 1986   [Fic]   86-20049
ISBN 0-395-41553-5

Printed in the United States of America

P 10 9 8 7 6 5 4 3 2 1

This one is for Steve,
who will always tell better jokes.
Sincere thanks to Anne, Elizabeth, Evan,
Siobhan, and Paul for comments and suggestions
on an earlier version of this story.

Contents

Follow That Mom!

1.

The Kid in the Middle

Basically, being the middle kid stinks. My mother keeps telling me I'm the lucky one, because I have an older sister to show me the ropes and a younger brother to look up to me. Sure. What it means is I have one to boss me around and one to tag after me. What kind of luck is that?

Don't get me wrong. I like Jeff and Karen — sort of. But don't fall for that line about one to show you the ropes and one to look up to you. My sister is treated like royalty because she's thirteen and the oldest and my brother gets away with murder because he's the baby. All I get in the middle is crowded — and yelled at.

Like this morning.

Jeff and I were talking about community helpers. Jeff had wanted to know if our dad was a community helper, because he had to give a report and all the good helpers, like firefighters and police officers, were taken already. My brother is nervous about passing kindergarten.

I said, "Sure, Dad is a community helper. He helps people with their computers. Moms can be community helpers, too. Fran's mom is a community helper. She teaches history at the high school. And Jennifer's mom. She sells houses. And Bonnie's mom. She's a dentist." I was really rolling. "Just about everybody is a community helper," I said.

"What does our mom do?" said Jeff.

"Our mom?" I had to stop and think about that one.

"Well," I said finally, "Mom doesn't do anything. She's a community helper just by being our mother."

Jeff understood, but Mom sure didn't. She came screeching around the corner to the breakfast nook, sloshing orange juice from the glass in her hand and her eyes spitting lasers.

"What do you mean, Maxine Goode, by *that* remark?"

(It's Goode as in good, not Goode as in goody-goody. That, by the way, is me, Maxine Butler Goode, which shortened is Maxine B. Goode. My parents definitely have a sick sense of humor. Eleven years old. Sixth grade. Five feet two, eyes of blue, and soon to be blasted into subatomic particles.)

"Remark? *Me* make remarks?" I said.

"I do something. I am doing something right now! I am mixing your brownies for the Sixth Grade Bake Sale. I am finding Jeff's left sneaker, and in less than one hour I will have walked Arf, dropped off your father's suit at the cleaner's, I will have argued with the manager of Grand's Department Store about their broken-down dishwashers, and, furthermore, I will have won!"

"Gee, Mom. You're a community helper. But not like Bonnie's mom, that's all. Or Jennifer's mom. Or Fran's mom. Just not like that."

Jeff would have to add his two cents. "Or like Christopher's mom. She's the crossing guard."

Mom's face turned purple-red. "That does it!"

She gave us this big lecture about how she could have been somebody important by now. Then she dragged a warped, moldy scrapbook from a warped, moldy box in the basement. It was from college, when she had a different name and her picture was in the paper for winning class treasurer.

Mom talked at us so long she had to drive Jeff and me to school in her bathrobe.

Mom still wasn't over it at lunchtime. She asked Jeff if he'd be happier if she got a job. Jeff was all for it. He wanted her to be a cowboy. And if she couldn't do that, he wanted her to be a fighter pilot.

Then she asked me. Would I be happier if she got a job? I mean, really, how should I know? So I said I didn't care much one way or the other.

Some days you can't win. I was late to school again.

After that I came home in the afternoon and

headed straight for my room before Mom could see me. Then I remembered: I didn't have a room anymore.

I sat on the floor in the upstairs hallway and stared at my old door. I could hear Dad's computer keys clicking away behind it. I used to have a whole set of Glow-in-the-Dark decals glued to that door. They were great when you had to get a drink of water in the middle of the night.

A couple of months ago my dad quit his job and started his own business at our house. He needed an office for the corporation and I had to move into Queen Karen's room because hers was bigger. Karen is in eighth grade and she thinks she's a queen. She wouldn't let me put up my Glow-in-the-Darks, not even on the ceiling, because of her snooty friends. She didn't want her snooty friends to think they belonged to her.

I don't know what my mother had to be mad about. She didn't get kicked out of her own room.

I was making faces at the corporation, daring my father to open it, when Queen Karen bounced up the stairs. She always bounces. She thinks it's popular to be peppy.

"Oh, I get it. You're practicing smiling," she said and smirked as if she'd made some hilarious remark. I gave her my special Ugly Face for Jerky Sisters. I liked Karen better when I had my own room. Now if I'm mad at her I don't have any place to go, except to my friend Bonnie Silver's.

Bonnie is my attorney. That's really a lawyer, but Bonnie wants me to call her an attorney. She says it sounds better, because lawyers have a bad name. By third grade I knew I needed one, whatever you call it. I think every kid should have a lawyer. Especially me. So I asked Bonnie.

Bonnie said she'd try it. She watches a lot of *Lone Ranger* reruns and *People's Court* on TV. We haven't had any trials yet. Mostly Bonnie writes letters. She wrote one to *Sports Illustrated* about how they never have articles on karate. I want to learn karate, so I can scare the wits and many other things out of Queen Karen.

The time I found Honey Jumbos cereal mixed in with my box of Puff'ems, Bonnie threatened to sue the company. They sent a whole carton of Puff'ems, free.

Right now Bonnie's working on a letter to the board of education because our teacher, Miss Halibut, told me I can't wear my baseball cap with the Mean Maxine buttons in school. Mean Maxine is a lady wrestler. Miss Halibut says there's no such thing as a *lady* wrestler. I don't care. She looks like a lady to me.

Mean Maxine is plastered on all my stuff. There's a great store downtown called Abe's Label's where you can have anything you want printed on T-shirts and buttons and stickers. You can get these monsters, like a lady's head with snakes crawling in her hair, or a sea creature with fourteen eyes, but Mean Maxine is my favorite.

Miss Halibut and Mom both say the Mean Maxine shirts show I have a bad attitude. But I like it that there's a wrestler with the same name as mine.

The town council tried to outlaw Mr. Label's store. They couldn't because of free speech. If the store can have free speech, I should have free speech, too. Such as on my baseball cap.

That night, dinner was leftover chicken and broccoli rolled up in white things fixed to look like pancakes. Only Mom didn't fool me. I knew what she was hiding inside. She sat there with her iceberg look, daring me to complain. She could freeze hot dogs with her iceberg look.

Then Mom announced she was going to be doing something — capital D, capital S. "From now on there may be many nights when you'll have to eat leftovers, or else make your own sandwiches," she said. "Jeff can make peanut butter and jelly, can't you, Jeff?" She looked pretty smug about it, if you ask me.

"What do you mean, Jean?" Dad asked.

Mom answered in her fake lollipop voice. "Ohh, nothing much, dear. It's just that the children are older and I need to find some things to do" —

(Translation: "Remember *that* remark, Maxine?")
— "so I'll feel I'm contributing."

"You mean a job, Jean?"

"Not exactly," my mother cooed.

(Brother, can she put it on. She should have been an actress in one of those soap operas Queen Karen watches.)

"I won't be paid, but it will be the same as a part-time job, and I'll have meetings to attend."

"Great, but what is it?"

"You'll see," said Mom, and she flashed all her teeth. "I want it to be a surprise. In the meantime, just don't expect your usual fancy dinners." She made a point of winking at me.

As I said, she can put it on. I figured that's all it was, an act to make me feel crummy for saying she didn't do anything. I tried to make it up to her. I remembered to say thank you for the leftovers and I complimented her on her dusting for a couple of days, and then I forgot about it.

2.

Surprise!

A couple of weeks later we had our first Girl Scout meeting of the school year. Bonnie and I walked to the band room together. We had to walk slowly because every finger and every toe we owned was crossed. We were hoping that when we opened the band room door Ruth Ellen Wolfe wouldn't be there.

Ruth Ellen Wolfe is in our grade, only she tries to act a lot older. She wears stockings and lip gloss and hangs out at the water fountain by the gym so the boys will fall over dead of thirst. Ruth Ellen's ambition in life is to be a popular like my sister Karen. I'd rather have a good hook shot.

Unfortunately, her mother and my mother are best friends. My mother is always trying to get Ruth Ellen and me together. She says Ruth Ellen has social skills. She wishes some of them would rub off on me.

Ruth Ellen's mother is our Scout leader. Mrs. Wolfe by herself is okay. I mean, she can't help it if her daughter is turning out to be a conceited snob, but, lately, having Ruth Ellen in the troop was really wrecking things. All she and her friends wanted to do was fold napkins for their Hospitality badge or square dance. Our troop hadn't been to Camp Wocka Wocka in months.

Patty Ryan told me that her mother had told her that Ruth Ellen wanted to quit Scouts. (Mrs. Ryan used to be our co-leader, until she had another baby.) I would have asked Ruth Ellen, but Ruth Ellen and I aren't on looking-at-each-other terms, let alone speaking-to-each-other terms.

If twenty fingers and twenty toes won't make your wish come true, nothing will, I thought, as Bonnie and I limped down the basement corridor to the meeting. "This troop isn't big enough for both of us," I said. "One of us has to go."

"But what about her mother?" said Bonnie.

"What about her?"

"Ruth Ellen can't quit if her mother doesn't quit."

I hadn't thought about Ruth Ellen's mother. "Well, Mrs. Wolfe could stay if she wanted to."

"And not have your own kid in your own troop? That looks kind of bad for business." Bonnie plinked the wires on her braces. "Why do you think I had to get these?"

"So you wouldn't look bad for business?"

Bonnie nodded.

My feet were starting to cramp. "Shut up, Bonnie," I grumbled. "Don't confuse me with facts." Bonnie always complicates things. It's an annoying habit lawyers have.

We stopped at the band room. "It's either her or me," I said.

"Open it."

"Don't rush me." I wanted to make sure we had given all those crossed fingers and toes enough time to work.

I opened the door a sliver and peeked in. When I didn't see Ruth Ellen, I started feeling braver. I edged inside. "I don't think she's here."

"Who isn't?" someone behind me demanded. I froze. "Oh, it's you," the voice continued. "How are you, wart? As warty as ever?"

I turned and faced Ruth Ellen. "I — I thought you quit."

"You lucked out, wart. I'm sticking around. Mother's rules — no Girl Scouts, no teen telephone. The things I have to put up with," she said and flounced into the meeting room.

Bonnie and I looked at each other. "The things her mother has to put up with," I said.

We watched Ruth Ellen giggling in a corner with her biggest hanger-on-er, darling Darlene. "What do we do now?" I asked.

"We quit," answered Bonnie. "What else?"

"Sure, what else." I was feeling glum all of a

sudden. I'd miss these dingy basement walls and pipes.

But I wouldn't miss Ruth Ellen.

Mrs. Wolfe was clapping her hands and sweeping the girls into a circle in the middle of the room. "Girls! Girls! Your attention, please. I have a very special announcement to make. As you know, Mrs. Ryan had to resign —"

Bonnie and I sneaked toward the exit. "Good riddance to you, too, Ruthie," I whispered. We were just about out the door — when there I was, face-to-face with my mother — MY MOTHER — dressed in a green lady Girl Scout uniform. What was she doing *here* dressed like *that*? Unless —

I screamed. I couldn't help myself. I'm not the kind of person who is good at surprises.

My mother looked at me. "I thought you'd be pleased, dear."

My mother, a Girl Scout leader? My mother, who has never been inside a sleeping bag in her life? Who thinks cooking out means buying fast food and eating it at the picnic table? My mother, who thinks hiking means high heels?

I glanced down at my knee pads and basketball hightops, then at my mother's feet. There they were. "You'll have to trade in your stilts, Mom." Heh heh. I could see her on the Palisades in those jobbies. She'd hike herself right into the Hudson River.

"Oh, those," she said. "Of course, I'll have boots for outdoors. I thought I could make a contribution, Maxine."

"Oh sure, Mom. That's a great idea." (What's a fib between relatives?)

"Then you don't mind?"

"Mind?" (I'm not stupid. Even I know you don't tell your mother you can't stand her best friend's daughter, especially in front of her best friend. I want to live.)

"The way you screamed just now, I thought —"

"Oh that. I always scream when I come down here. This is the room they use for the spook house for the school's annual Halloween party. Every time I come in here I remember what it was like — the chills crowding up my spine, the ghoulish faces. Hard to shake off an experience like that. I mean, it's only been — what? — maybe eleven months since the last Halloween party. It takes time to recover. Bonnie says I could sue — for mental deterioration."

I backpedaled into the meeting room. My mother wasn't the only one who could put on an act.

Most of the meeting Ruth Ellen had all the other girls except Bonnie and Patty Ryan and me slobbering over her, and Patty Ryan looked as if she wished she were. The one time Ruth Ellen looked down she pointed at my Mean Maxine shirt and said, "What's *that* supposed to be?"

"*That* is my favorite shirt," I answered. As if she didn't know.

"A popular wouldn't be caught dead in anything like *that*."

"Good, because I wouldn't be caught alive in anything a popular wears."

"What are you? A geek?"

"No. A normal."

Naturally, Mom tried right away to push Ruth Ellen and me together. Ruth Ellen's mother was teaching us some new knots. (Mrs. Wolfe has this hang-up about knots.) Mom nudged. "Ask Ruth Ellen to help you." And when I refused, *she* asked Ruth Ellen.

The first chance I had, I cornered Bonnie. "You're my lawyer. Help!"

"Tell her on the way home."

"Tell my mother we were going to quit?"

"You have to. It's the only way," said Bonnie.

"You're right. I have to," I repeated, but I didn't like the worried look on Bonnie's face.

Bonnie promised to call me afterward on her CB walkie-talkie. She pretended she had some errand or other so that Mom and I could ride home alone.

I never did dream up a clever way to break the news to Mom so she wouldn't be mad, because as soon as we were in the car, she said, "Where were you and Bonnie going when I arrived at the meeting?" The way she said it I guessed my little act hadn't fooled her. This wasn't polite curiosity. This was suspicion.

I tried to be casual. "Oh — home."

"Home?"

"Yeah. Home."

"Aren't you feeling well?"

I blurted it out. "I felt fine until I saw Ruth Ellen Wolfe. She makes me sick. That's why I was leaving."

"Maxine! That's a terrible thing to say."

"Sometimes the truth is a terrible thing to say. I want to quit Girl Scouts, Mom. I have to quit. Before I die of toxic waste. Ruth Ellen is toxic and she's a waste."

"Quit?" Mom laughed one of those laughs that meant she didn't think this was funny. "Because of Ruth Ellen Wolfe? Don't be ridiculous."

"We could be ridiculous together. You could quit, too."

"I just joined."

"Okay, I'll be ridiculous by myself."

"No."

"Please?"

"I'm not quitting and you're not quitting." She patted me on the knee. "I'm glad I'll be available to help you work this thing out. Some day you'll appreciate Ruth Ellen. In the meantime, you have to learn to get along with all kinds of people, Maxine."

"What if I go insane?"

"No," Mom said firmly.

Rats.

3.

"Masked Man to Mean Maxine"

Mom and I arrived home and I ran upstairs to wait
for Bonnie to call. Queen Karen and her best friend
Fawn were in our bedroom playing Teen-ager.
Teen-ager means they put on lipstick and eyeshadow
and spray the room with a quart of perfume. Then
Karen gets on the extension phone and they pretend
they're talking to boys. Karen gets to be the girl first
and Fawn is the boy. Fawn's a sap: she does whatever Karen tells her.

I asked Dad if I could wait in the corporation
closet. The reception on the walkie-talkie was always better in my old room anyway. He didn't mind.
Bonnie says it's important for an attorney to be in
constant contact with her clients. That's why she let
me have one of her walkie-talkies. For emergencies.
This certainly was an emergency.

"Masked Man to Mean Maxine. Masked Man to
Mean Maxine. Over."

"Hi-yo, Silver," I answered in a whisper.

"Where are you? Over."

"I've left the divided queendom." (That's code for Karen's and my bedroom.) "I'm in the corporate dungeon. Can I visit the judge's chambers?" (That's code for Bonnie's house.) "I need a personal consultation to review the case. Urgent. Over."

"Negative. Over." (No means yes, and yes means no. We do that so anyone who's listening in won't know what we're saying.)

Bonnie's house is right behind ours. Bonnie's mother was stirring a huge pot of spaghetti sauce for the freezer when I got there. "Next's week's dinners," she said. Mrs. Silver makes awesome spaghetti, but Bonnie hates it when she cooks for the freezer. It means a whole week of whatever it was she made. I wouldn't mind. At least you'd know what's for dinner and somebody isn't trying to sneak you fake pancakes.

Mrs. Silver waved her ladle. "Bonnie's in the den."

The Silvers' house is real big and has a lot of empty rooms. Mrs. Silver says it saves on cleaning. It's a little creepy. Your voice echoes. But the den is great. There's a remote control and a gigantic couch with tons of puffy pillows and cushions to hold your head right to see TV.

Bonnie was watching a *Lone Ranger* rerun. She turned the TV off. I like it when Bonnie turns off the tube to talk, because then I know she's not half-listening to something else at the same time she half-listens to me. (Like some conceited sisters I know.) Bonnie offered me some pretzels. "What did she say?"

"She said N–O, no." I flopped on the couch. "I can't quit Scouts. According to my mother, Ruth Ellen isn't a good enough reason. I should have known it was going to be a rotten-luck day. Arf found my rabbit's foot this morning and buried it in the back yard. He thought it was his doggie bone. The next thing I know my mother will be offering Ruth Ellen rides to school and inviting her over, and —" The possibilities were too awful to consider.

Bonnie munched on a pretzel. "Ruth Ellen will never quit. Not with a teen phone at stake. We have to get your mother to quit. Then you can quit."

"She says she just joined."

"What if we think of a way to make it so your mother is too busy to be a Scout leader?" said Bonnie. "That's the excuse my mom gives. Maybe we could find her a job." Bonnie's eyes widened. "Hey! The receptionist in my mother's office is moving to California."

"Too late. I already told my mother I didn't care if she got a job." I shook my head, remembering that day. Miss Halibut had said that anybody who was tardy twice in the same day wasn't mature enough to go out for recess. "Besides, she thinks being a Scout leader *is* a job. You should have heard her on the way home. She has leader lessons tonight.

She was so happy you would have thought she was going to Weight Watchers and she'd lost ten pounds. One meeting and she knows more knots than I do."

Bonnie had a strange twitch in her eye. "If we got her a baby she'd be too busy."

"Bonnie, how could we get my mother a baby, for crying out loud?"

"Not a people baby." Bonnie's eye was quivering very fast now. "An animal baby. A six-foot, eighty-pound, dog baby. A Great Dane!" Bonnie squealed. "My dad knew a guy once who had a Great Dane and he had a nervous breakdown."

"The owner?"

"No, the dog. The guy was very busy taking the dog to the dog therapist and trying to teach him not to be paranoid. The dog thought everyone hated him. He kept running away and the owner had to go to court because his Dane was violating the leash laws. It was a very interesting case. The dog's lawyer tried to use the insanity plea."

"I want my mother to quit Girl Scouts, not have a nervous breakdown." Bonnie can get carried away sometimes.

Bonnie was tapping her braces. This is another of her annoying habits. Bonnie's eyes rolled up into her eyebrows. I know that look. It means *watch out!* Oh goody, I thought. I was salivating over this idea I hadn't even heard yet. "So what is it?" I urged.

Bonnie came out of her trance and rubbed her hands together. I rubbed mine together, too. Oh boy. Oh boy. "You have to make her hate Girl Scouts," she whispered.

I slumped against the pillows.

"Think of something she really hates," said Bonnie.

That wasn't hard. "Noise. She's always telling us we make too much noise. Especially now that my dad has his office at home."

"So?"

"So — what?"

"It's simple. You make a *lot* of noise at Girl Scout meetings. The noise vibrates. Like a drill. In and out of her head." Bonnie's body shook. "She decides Girl Scouts is too noisy. She can't stand it." I pictured Mrs. Silver working on my mother with a giant drill like a jackhammer. That would do it all right. "She quits. You quit. And everybody lives happily ever after."

"She'll kill me."

"Not if she doesn't blame you for the noise."

"How do I do that?"

"You'll come up with something," said Bonnie.

Good thing Bonnie was confident, because I sure wasn't. All of a sudden I felt panicky. "You wouldn't do something like quit Girl Scouts without me."

"No way. You're my best friend."

"Thanks, Bonnie."

That night, before we went to sleep, Mom gave Karen and me keys to the house. She said she'd be going to a lot more of these Girl Scout training meetings and she didn't want us stranded outside in case she was late and Dad wasn't here to let us in.

Then she gave us her responsibility lecture, which basically says if you goof up on this one your mother will still love you, but you're probably going to be a lousy adult.

I groaned and pulled my baseball cap down over my eyes. I didn't want to hear any more. First I had to move out of my room and share a room with Queen Karen. Then Mom joins Girl Scouts and I'm stuck with Ruth Ellen Wolfe. Now my adult life depends on whether or not I lose this bitty hunk of metal. Who wouldn't have a bad attitude?

4.

Wud Ith Dis?

At breakfast Mom was bubbling about a dumb trip our Scout troop would be taking next week to visit a dumb submarine parked in the dumb Hackensack River. "The submarine's called the U.S.S. *Ling.* She's a World War II vessel. I suggested it at the meeting last night," my mother said proudly.

"I don't care if it's from the Revolutionary War. I'm not getting on any Ding-a-ling—"

Mom's neck and bottom lip went stiff. "Submarines did not exist in the Revolutionary War."

I said it louder. "I'm not getting on any DING-A-LING, and especially not with Ruth Ellen Wolfe."

"You spend too much time with Bonnie. You need to expand socially, learn some leadership skills." Mom whipped out one of her cream puff smiles. "I think Ruth Ellen is an excellent influence."

Why is it that the kid your mother *loves* is the person you absolutely can't stand?

"I'd like to learn how to lead myself right out of the troop," I muttered.

"What's that?"

"I said Bonnie is my lawyer. I have to spend a lot of time with her."

Then Jeff, who had been busy slurping orange juice through a straw, bragged, "I can come to the *Ling* and I'm not a Green Scout."

"You? If Jeff goes," I bawled, "and Ruth Ellen goes, my Mean Maxine shirt goes."

Whenever we have an argument Dad bangs on the pipes upstairs to make us stop. "Take it easy on my ex-radiator," I shouted back.

"All right," Mom whispered through her teeth, "I'll find a babysitter. No Mean Maxine shirt. Understand? Scout uniforms only."

Queen Karen strutted in. She was combing her hair as usual. It beats me how she has any hair left to comb. At Karen's school all the populars do during lunch is brush each other's hair. They'd rather brush than eat.

"By the way," said Karen, "your walkie-talkie is going crazy. Bonnie's outside waiting in the bushes. You, my dear, are going to be THE utter bottom — the UNpopular of the UNpopulars — if you keep hanging out with that two-legged antenna with a law library." Queen Karen gave one last, long brushstroke, as she disappeared out the door. "So long, Mother. 'Bye, ferd."

Maybe you haven't noticed. Populars are very good at dreaming up names for us normals. It's the only thing they're good at. (Besides combing.)

What I wished I could do was grab Karen's brush and smush it around in Jeff's oatmeal. She'd be cleaning her hair for days. But I stopped myself, or Bonnie would be waiting in the bushes until her batteries died.

On our way to school I told Bonnie about the trip to the *Ling.* "We've got to get my mother out, Bonnie." I pounded my fist. "If I spend too much time around Ruth Ellen it could ruin my personality."

I noticed Bonnie's eyes were rolling. "What's that about, Bonnie? You have an idea?"

"I can't tell." Bonnie squeezed her eyes tight. "It feels like an idea. Right behind my nose. But it doesn't look like one yet."

"Oh." I shrugged. "I want you to sue my mother," I went on.

"For what?" Bonnie opened her eyes.

"For not letting me wear my Mean Maxine shirt to the *Ling.*"

"You can't sue your mother for being motherly. Apple pie and motherhood, those are the two things you can't sue." Bonnie only takes cases she knows she can win.

"How about for slavery? Girl Scouts is supposed to be for people who want to join, right?"

"Hmmm. Involuntary membership. I'll look it up in my law books. You might be able to get her on that."

"We, Bonnie. We. You want to quit, too. Remember?" I was beginning to think Bonnie wasn't working hard enough on this problem. I could see the headlines now: ELEVEN-YEAR-OLD LOSES COURT BATTLE TO RESIGN SCOUT TROOP. MOTHER'S LAST MINUTE PLEA SWAYS JUDGE.

"Well, look at it this way," said Bonnie. "You probably won't have to be a Girl Scout when you go to college."

I groaned.

Later that morning we were lining up for recess. Miss Halibut asked for volunteers to stay in and clean erasers. Ruth Ellen Wolfe always gets picked, but she had already been picked to deliver messages for the principal. Bonnie's hand shot into the air and whirled like a propeller. "Raise your hand," she hissed at me.

"Huh?" Bonnie knows what happens when I clean erasers; the dust makes me sneeze. I erupt like Old Faithful, every fifteen seconds. Either Bonnie liked to watch people suffer or she had a good reason. I figured I might as well find out. I waved my hand, too.

The eraser-cleaning machine is in a small room off the gym. What you do is press the dusty side of the eraser down on this brush. That makes the brush whir and the chalk dust is sucked away into a bag at the end. If you push down hard, after a while the eraser starts to smell like sneakers that have been left in the dryer too long. Miss Halibut says erasers don't erase well with the burn marks. Everybody tries to hold them down long enough to make burn marks anyway.

I stood in the doorway while Bonnie jammed the erasers against the brush. "Come on in," said Bonnie.

"I can't."

"How can I be your lawyer if you won't let me advise you?"

"Advise me long distance. Have you got an idea or what, Bonnie?"

"Maybe. But you won't know what it is until you stand right here." Bonnie patted the chalk bag at the far end of the machine. Puffs of white dust billowed around the bag. It almost made me sneeze just to watch it.

"Can you sue your lawyer for bad advice?" I asked, inching into the room.

"Sure, but you'd have to find a new lawyer first." Bonnie jumped behind me and slammed the door closed. Whack! Whack! Clouds of dust filled the air.

Quick. Which was it to stop a sneeze? Look *at* the light? Or *away* from the light? I couldn't remember. My nose tickled, my eyes began to tear. My head whipped forward and back. KER-*CHOO*!

A few seconds later I sneezed again. And again. KER-*CHOO*! KER-*CHOO*! The sneezes bouncing back and forth made my ears ring.

Bonnie looked very proud of herself. "See?"

"See what?" I held my nose tight.

"This." Bonnie pried my fingers from my nose, which brought on a second round of head-cracking sneezes.

I clapped my hand on my nose again. "What is *this*?" It sounded as if I was saying, "Wud ith *dis*?" That's the way I sound when my allergies are bad.

"Noise! Your mother hates noise. I've been on the *Ling* before. It's tiny, like this room." Bonnie swung her arms to show how tiny. She could practically touch both walls at the same time. "Your mother can't blame you for an allergy attack, even if it is very noisy," she said gleefully.

"Where am I gonna find chalk dust on a submarine?"

"Easy." Bonnie picked up two bags of chalk dust and handed them to me.

"Steal them?"

"It's not stealing. Nobody needs chalk dust. The janitor throws it away. Think of it as recycling." Bonnie grinned, rocking back and forth on her heels.

While Bonnie finished cleaning erasers, I practiced tossing a couple of them into the basketball hoop in the gym. One stuck between the rim and the backboard. Bonnie and I threw tons of erasers at it, but we couldn't knock it down.

Miss Halibut would start wondering what happened to us, so we gave up and hid the bags of chalk dust in the bottom of the eraser bucket. Once we were in the classroom we put them in my book bag and ran outside for the rest of recess.

Boy, was it a relief to let go of my nose finally.

5.

Ding the *Ling*

Tuesday was *Ling* day. You could tell Mom was nervous about the trip. Dad was late to the "Y" pool to swim laps and Mom handed *him* Karen's lunch tickets and Karen the car keys. Karen loved that.

Meanwhile, Jeff was tossing Puff'ems in the air and catching them with his mouth. Good old Arf caught more than Jeff did. Mom acted as if she couldn't see it. She gets blind like that whenever she's nervous. I had my uniform on and she must have asked me twenty times, where was it. Finally I stopped telling her.

These were good signs. When Mom's rattled, noise sends her straight up the wall. Express. I was feeling so terrific I aced Miss Halibut's spelling test, even though Miss Halibut tries to trick us by pronouncing the words as if she's sucking on a sourball.

After school I was standing in the parking lot waiting for our car. I checked my sleeves. Bonnie had fastened the rubber bands that held the chalk bags in place sort of tight and my arms were starting to ache. I wiggled one of them loose.

Just then our yellow station wagon pulled into the lot. There was my brother in the front seat beside my mother. Something must have happened to Mrs. Aiello, Jeff's babysitter. This was definitely a piece of luck, because Jeff's the world's best noisemaker. We could package him and sell him for New Year's Eve. But I figured I'd better squawk about his coming, or Mom would catch on.

"Hey, Jeffy," I yelled, "what are *you* doing here?"

"Mrs. Jello has arf-er-itis, so I have to come. I'm a Green Scout for the day. Mommy says." Jeff nodded yes and looked v-e-r-y important.

"Did Arf bite her?"

"Arthritis," my mother answered. "Mrs. Aiello's having another attack. She can't sit for Jeff today."

"Yeah, arf-er-itis."

"You have to learn to roll with the punches, dear." Dear is my mother's pet name for me. She thinks if she calls me Dear I'll behave.

I glared at Jeff as I climbed in the back and slammed the door to make it look good. "You're not a Green Scout. Or a Girl Scout. You're a pipsqueak."

My mother smiled her crocodile smile — all teeth. "Thank you for cooperating, dear."

By now Mrs. Wolfe had arrived in her car. The other girls straggled out to the parking lot.

Half the troop piled in our wagon. Including
Ruth Ellen Wolfe. I would have wangled a ride in
the other car, but I was itching to start this noise
campaign. All day Bonnie had been slipping me
notes: NOISE ANNOYS. BLAST AWAY AND
BUST OUT. DING THE LING.

As soon as the car started, I was belting out Girl
Scout songs at the top of my lungs. Lucky for me,
Ruth Ellen joined in. My mother HATES singing
and whistling in the car. She says she can't drive.
But she could hardly object to Scout songs, right?
Especially if they were popular, and Ruth Ellen
wouldn't do anything unless it was popular.

I could tell it was getting to her. Mom's eyebrows
looked as if they were growing together.

I turned up the volume.

"On top of spaghetti, all covered with cheese,
 I lost my poor meatball when somebody sneezed..."

By the time we climbed out of the car in Hackensack, Mom was as jumpy as a kangaroo. I was feeling a little woozy myself but it was worth it. Just
to make sure I screamed. "WAKE UP!!"

Mom gasped and clutched the neck of her coat.
She practically strangled herself. Ruth Ellen turned
and looked at me as if I were a Martian.

"Heh heh. My foot fell asleep," I said.

We had to wait for our tour guide in a squatty
building next to the parking lot. There was a little

kids' birthday party going on, kids about Jeff's size. Jeff was so interested in the party he nearly burned his nose on the candles.

The rest of us tried not to look at the food too much. We stared at a lot of pictures of water on the walls. The only good one was of a guy from Paterson who built the first submarine. The first submarine looked like a watermelon.

Bonnie and I hid behind a screen covered with pictures of ships and did a chalk-dust check. The bags were still there.

Finally our guide came and we could board the *Ling*. He looked like some sort of officer. He led us across the metal deck and down the hatch into the submarine, the cleats on his black shoes click-clicking across the deck.

The U.S.S. *Ling* must have been made for human sardines. The passages were so cramped we had to walk single file and duck our heads in order not to bang the pipes. And everything was metal, exactly as Bonnie promised. Walls, pipes, doors, steps, and floors. Metal was best, Bonnie said, for making noise.

We were squashed together in the torpedo room. I squeezed around behind Bonnie and stood next to my mother and Jeff. I wiggled a pinky finger inside my left sleeve and punched a small hole into the chalk bag.

"This cubby is where the ship's radio operator worked," the guide said.

I pretended to have an itch and rubbed my nose with my sleeve. Meanwhile I took a good whiff. We were walking forward to another part of the submarine.

"This is where the crew slept. You will notice there are only one-third as many bunks as I mentioned there were crewmen. That's to save on space. Every eight hours a different shift used the bunks. The men had a hard time falling asleep until someone discovered that it was because the sheets were warm. Now after his watch, every man brought his own sheets and made up his bunk," I heard the guide say.

Something was wrong. Nothing was happening. This time I poked the bag with my thumb.

My nostrils began to curl and the guide was turning fuzzy around the edges. I sniffed. Again. My lungs decided to go down fighting. Wheeze. Cough. Ah-AH-*CHOO*!

The guide talked louder. "THIS IS THE GALLEY."

My mother scowled and handed me a tissue.

"Must be dusty in here," I said. "Old submarine." I gulped more chalky air when she wasn't looking. "Ah-AH-*CHOO*!" My mother handed me a wad of tissue. She was turning into a crocodile again.

All of a sudden a KER-*CHOO* blasted me from behind. It had to be a whale.

No, it was Mrs. Wolfe. I didn't know she was allergic, too.

Mrs. Wolfe had dropped her purse. We both bent over to pick it up — when it happened. We sneezed at the same time. KA-BOOM! We whacked heads. I was vibrating like a Chinese gong. I threw my arms to catch myself.

A stream of chalk dust flew out from one sleeve and a bag from the other. The stream of dust — by now it was a river — landed all over Mrs. Wolfe's clothes. The bag popped her in the kisser and exploded. The stuff hung off her chin, off her nose. Globs of it hung off her eyebrows. She looked like a dried-up cream pie.

Other people started sneezing. About then I heard a metal tinkling sound. My back door key!

I dropped to the floor and crawled toward the sound. I thought I had it, but every time I sneezed I lost it again in a white cloud.

Jeff crawled behind me. "I love being a Green Scout," he sang. "I wanna be one forever."

That is, until we tried to scoot between the wrong pair of legs. These were unmistakably Mom's legs. I could tell because she pinched her knees together and wouldn't let us pass. I looked up. She wasn't a crocodile anymore. She was a Tyrannosaurus Rex. An albino Tyrannosaurus Rex.

On the way home, in between sneezes, I fired Bonnie.

Later that night she called me. Snap. Crackle. Bleep. "Masked Man to Mean Maxine. Are you there? Over."

Silence.

"Masked Man to Mean Maxine. I know you're there. Over."

Bonnie was right. I was there. I was sitting in the corporation closet with the walkie-talkie turned on, just to listen to her squirm.

"Masked Man to Mean Maxine. Am I still fired? Over."

A *long* silence.

"What do you think?" I said. I was breathing through my mouth because my nose was so stuffy. "Over."

"I knew you were there. What did your mother say? Over."

" 'No self-respecting person pours chalk dust all over Ruth Ellen Wolfe's mother.' "

"Uh-oh."

"My mother — my own mother — is going to report me to the principal for stealing chalk dust."

"I guess I'm still fired. Over."

"I guess you are." I blew my nose again. "Over."

"For how long?"

"Till my allergy goes away!" I shouted. The CB crackled and went dead.

6.

Glow-in-the-Darks

My punishment for stealing the chalk dust was cleaning erasers every day for a week — after school, naturally — so for a week straight I hung onto my nose. Whenever Miss Halibut just swiped at the board my eye sockets felt as if they had blown a fuse.

I was also locked out of the house all week. No key. Karen arranged it so she'd be at her slave Fawn's house practicing cheerleading after school. That's something else the populars do: jump up and down at the junior high football games to show off their underwear.

Karen would come home and see me waiting for her and really rub it in. She'd wave her key and talk way up high in that gummy voice she uses when she's playing Teen-ager.

By Friday I wasn't going to give her the satisfaction, not after cleaning seventy-six erasers. Jeff was at Mrs. Aiello's. My mother was at her second meeting on how to build campfires. (Her first campfire fizzled. She didn't know about tinder.) And I don't know where my dad was supposed to be.

I decided to stand over by Bonnie's back door (no one was home there either) where I could watch our house and sort of appear when Karen did.

Except Queen Karen beat me to it. She was sitting on Bonnie's back steps when I got there. The rat. She smiled her rubbing-it-in smile. "I'm surprised you weren't home hours ago."

"I'm surprised you're not bald," I said, and I dashed for our house. I tried all the doorknobs, praying one had been left unlocked, but no such luck, and a few moments later I heard a slam in back. I rang the front doorbell until my thumb was numb to make sure Queen Karen knew I hated her.

Finally Dad drove up.

"Hey, Dad," I said after he had opened the back door and we were both safely in, "you think I could visit my old room for a few minutes?"

"I was planning to work before dinner, Max." He tried to sound stern because he knew Mom would want him to be. Then he looked at me a little sideways. "Anything wrong?"

Was he kidding? My nose had blisters from holding it so much, my sister had humiliated me, I'd lost all sensation in my hand from pressing the bell, and he asks is anything wrong.

"Nah," I said. "I just miss the old place. I could go in the closet," I offered.

"As long as you're quiet."

I brought my sticker book and a flashlight into the closet with me. Pretty soon the Glow-in-the-Darks were glowing. It used to smell of old sneakers in here. Now it didn't smell of anything. I missed the sneaker smell. Without it I couldn't pretend the room was mine and it was the good old days again.

What I needed was someone to talk to. Someone like Bonnie.

I tiptoed past Dad, way up high on my toes so he'd see I was trying not to disturb him, and tiptoed back with the walkie-talkie.

"Mean Maxine to Masked Man." I was hoping Bonnie was home from oboe lessons by now. On about the sixtieth try she answered. "I'm sorry I fired you, Bonnie," I said.

"I'm sorry, too. I mean about getting you into trouble. I was sure it would work. Honest."

"I guess we'd better think of something else. My mom always knows it's me making the noise."

"Yeah. I guess. Today was your last day cleaning erasers, wasn't it?"

"How did you know?"

"It's my job. I couldn't let Miss Halibut slip extra erasers in on you, or anything."

"You didn't stop being my lawyer, even though I fired you?"

"No."

I thought for a moment. "I didn't stop being your friend either."

"That's what I figured," said Bonnie. "Where are you?"

"I'm in the corporation closet."

"Don't move. I have something to show you."

"Wait! My dad—" But Bonnie had turned her walkie-talkie off.

A few minutes later I heard Dad say, "She's inside." Then I heard a rapping at the door. "Come in." It seemed a little strange to say come in, when it's a closet you're saying to come into, but I said it anyway.

Bonnie skootched next to me. She handed me something.

"What's this?"

"A mirror."

Then she handed me a small round thing with a hole in the middle. It had a chalky feel to it. (I know what chalk feels like.)

"Chew it with your mouth open and watch your teeth in the mirror," she said.

The whole thing seemed pretty strange to me, but Bonnie is like that. She'll tell you to do things, like chewing with your mouth open, that Queen Karen would kill you for. I held up the mirror and chewed. There wasn't much to see except the closet started to smell medicine-y. "What am I eating?"

"Wintergreen Life Savers."

All of a sudden tiny flares of light bounced off my teeth. "Hey! I'm a lightning bug!"

"Here. Try another one." It did it again.

Then Bonnie tried it, and then we both did it to see who could make the biggest flash. Chew. Chew. Chew. Ping!

Bonnie won. She stuck a bunch of Life Savers in her mouth at the same time and her teeth and braces all sparkled yellow-green.

"This is awesome," I said. "How did you find out about it?"

"I read it in a book my mom has, *Dental Wizardry: Tricks to Amaze Your Patients.*"

"Amazing."

Bonnie laughed. "See? It works."

Later Bonnie and I rode our bikes to Connelly's Corner Store and bought all the wintergreen Life Savers Mr. Connelly had. On the way back we stopped by the playground, then at Bonnie's.

Mrs. Silver was there mixing up a lot of hamburger. "What is it this week, Mrs. Silver?"

"Meatloaf."

"Yum."

Bonnie doubled over as if she had a bellyache. Her mother ignored her.

"I have more teeth for you, Maxine, if you're still interested." Mrs. Silver slapped the meat mixture into pans.

"Oh, no thank you, Mrs. Silver. I'm not making monster choppers lately." I didn't have the heart to tell her my mother wouldn't let me. Mrs. Silver had been so nice about giving us the teeth she pulled.

Bonnie and I used to make false teeth with this clay set I had. We pretended they were for dinosaurs and monsters. After the clay dried, we painted them. They looked as if they were dripping blood and purple ooze.

We left our best set once in the bathroom sink. Bonnie and I hid behind the shower curtain, waiting for Queen Karen. Queen Karen's face turned pure white. She grabbed her mouth and ran. She even forgot to comb her hair.

My mother threw the monster choppers out. That really made me mad, because some of the teeth were mine, ones I kept after I learned the truth about the tooth fairy.

"Mrs. Silver, what do you do when someone hates you and is always giving you a hard time?"

Mrs. Silver winked. "Like older sisters?"

Like older sisters — and older mothers, I thought.

"Well," said Mrs. Silver, popping seven meatloaf pans into the oven, "a situation like that calls for a little psychology. Changing someone's mind isn't easy. Especially in my business. Everyone dislikes the dentist. *Before* the dentist has done a thing."

I perked up. That was my problem exactly.

"They claim you can persuade people to like

something they dislike by associating it with things that are already pleasant to them."

(Huh?)

"So I used to give my patients candy and ice cream cones."

"Oh, you mean like a bribe."

"But then some of my mothers objected. If I gave them sweets, how could they tell their children the dentist says it is bad for them?" Mrs. Silver sighed. "Dentists want to be loved, too."

When I went home I gave my mother a pack of wintergreen Life Savers. I was trying to persuade her to like something she dislikes — me. Maybe *I'd* make a good dentist. I was used to having mothers hate me.

That night I hid the Life Savers under my pillow and told myself to wake up at 3:00 A.M. I just said it to myself and I woke up. My grandfather told me our bodies have a kind of clock inside and the way you set it is by saying to yourself, Wake up at such-and-such a time. The first time I tried it I was awake at three o'clock because I had been awake all night wondering if it would work or not, but the second time I tried it I woke up ten minutes early. Grandpa says our clocks are pretty good, but not accurate to the second or anything. I like the idea of a clock ticking away; it makes me feel like the crocodile in Peter Pan.

I found my Life Savers — (Tick Tick) — and

tiptoed over to Queen Karen. She had her smug rubbing-it-in look on her face (Tick Tick Tick). I threw a few wintergreens in my mouth. Then I jiggled her bed with my knee. She rolled onto her side and looked up (Tick Tick).

I bared my teeth. Ping ping. Ping-ping-ping!

Queen Karen lifted, straight as a rod. "HELP! MOTHER! DADDY!"

I zipped back under my covers as fast as I could and swallowed the Life Savers. A few seconds later Dad stumbled in, rubbing his eyes, "What is it?"

Karen was doing a dance on her bed. "I saw a monster. With green teeth. It was shooting sparks. Right there, right where you are now."

"Green teeth?" Dad mumbled.

"Yes! A flashing green monster!"

Dad came over to my bed. My eyes were clamped so tight I was seeing stars. He sniffed, then slipped a hand under my pillow and removed the last two rolls of Life Savers. I wondered how he knew about wintergreen Life Savers. "Good-bye to one week's allowance," he whispered beside my ear.

He was padding out of the room. Karen was still dancing on her bed. "You can get down, Karen. It was a bad dream. It won't happen again. (Pause.) I promise you."

Making Queen Karen scream was worth being locked out of the house and *two* weeks' allowance.

7.

A No-Cartoon Weekend

About the only one glad to see me get up Saturday morning was Arf. Good ol' Arf. He wagged his chubby tail and arfed, while everybody else stared into their cereal bowls. They were all so puckered and sour you would have thought someone dropped a giant pickle in their juice. While I ate, Mom gave me another lecture, this time on getting along with people and how I needed Girl Scouts to get along.

I was such a hit at breakfast I figured I'd better skip my Saturday cartoons. My parents like it when they think I'm giving up something to make up for a bad deed I did wrong. I always start small though. That way I can tell if it's just another no-cartoon weekend or if I have to sacrifice. You know: stay home and play with your baby brother, like that.

Dad came into the family room later. He saw the TV and grunted. I was watching the educational channel. "Okay," he said, "I won't dock your allowance this time. But no visits to the office until you apologize to your sister."

A no-cartoon weekend. But my Dad is always easy. Mom never settles for just cartoons. I wondered how much I'd have to give up to get her out of Girl Scouts.

Dad kept cruising through to check on how serious I was about being forgiven (probably for Mom), so I was stuck with watching a man in a pizza-shaped cap talking about some painter named Vincent.

They showed a picture of Vincent. He painted it himself. He had reddish hair and a pipe and a big bandage over his ear. I couldn't see what was so educational about Vincent, although I liked one of his pictures, the one of his yellow bedroom. Before it became the corporation my bedroom was yellow.

Too bad about Vincent's ear.

Vincent and my room were making me very depressed. I was thinking of calling Bonnie on the walkie-talkie to see if I could watch cartoons at her house, when the announcer started blabbing about a program on psychology. Introduction to psychology, he called it. "On next."

Hey! Didn't Mrs. Silver say I needed to use a little psychology? Maybe I didn't have to give up anything. I shinnied closer to the set and turned up the volume.

Well, to make a long program short, what I saw was a lot of white rats and pigeons in cages. The rats ran down these short hallways called mazes. A lady in a doctor coat like Mrs. Silver's thought it was pretty neat when they learned on the first try to turn left or right to get to the food box. (They taught worms to go left or right, too. Now *that* was neat, watching those little guys wiggle straight to the food box.)

The pigeons didn't have to run down hallways. They had to peck at dark squares and light squares, whichever was right. Then the lady in the white coat showed how she could make the pigeons turn around in circles.

The pigeon would be wandering around his box and the first time he turned his head a certain way — click — the lady would push the lever and drop a food pellet and the pigeon would run over to his dish and eat. Pigeons look pretty jerky when they hurry. Then the pigeon would go back and turn again, farther, and — click — another pellet, and more pellets, until he did a whole circle.

The lady said they never use punishment to train them, only rewards. I liked the part about using only rewards. My mother ought to learn a little psychology, too.

After the program I lay on my bed a long time, thinking. Queen Karen was trying out a new perfume and spraying like a skunk, so it wasn't easy — thinking, I mean.

On one hand, psychology was simple. You just hand out pellets. Enough pellets and my mother would do what I wanted her to do. She'd be in my power. Heh heh heh. She'd quit Girl Scouts whenever I said. I pretended I was Count Dracula moving in for the big bite.

There was one problem, however. What if my mother wouldn't eat?

My mother is one of those people who's always on a strict diet, so she's always hungry. But she won't eat, not unless she's just lost weight and then she eats like a — I almost said like a horse, but I don't know how a horse eats. Grandpa told me once a boa constrictor can swallow a cow. They swallow things whole. My mother eats like a boa constrictor. She could swallow a refrigerator whole when she thinks she's skinny.

But Mom hadn't lost any weight recently. Then I had an idea. The next time I had to use the bathroom I turned the knob on the bottom of the scales. I weighed myself. Presto! — six pounds gone. My mother would be so thrilled she'd never notice.

After I rigged the scales I started having this flip-floppy feeling, right above the button on my jeans. Maybe I should try this psychology stuff first. See if it works.

On what, I asked myself. And it hit me like a revolving door. Thud. Thud-thud-thud-thud.

Worms! There were a zillion of them behind the garage in Grandpa's compost heap. Compost is this yucchy mixture of leaves and garbage, like eggs and potato peels and coffee grounds, that you let sit around in a pile until it's incredibly wormy and then people use it in their gardens. Who'd want to eat carrots that came out of a garden with that gunk in it, I don't know, but worms go wild for the stuff.

Grandpa says he doesn't have enough garbage at his house to make a good compost heap, so Dad saves ours for him. Once in a while Grandpa comes over and stirs it up. The last time he came the compost was swimming with worms.

Grandpa wouldn't miss a few, I decided as I ran outside.

I scooped up a shovelful of compost and turned it over. What did I tell you — swimming with worms. It looked like an earthworm convention! I put back the fat, juicy ones and kept the skinny guys because they looked the hungriest. Then I dug a bunch of T-shaped trails in the back yard, like the mazes on the television show, and dropped a tablespoon of compost at the end of each T, after the right turn.

About then Bonnie showed up with her walkie-talkie. "I tried to call you. How can we be in constant communication if you don't have your walkie-talkie with you at all times?" She stopped. "What are you doing — practicing your alphabet?"

I guess I had gone overboard. There were T's everywhere on the lawn. "I'm training worms to go right or left," I said. I dropped a worm at the beginning of each maze. "So I can make my mother do what I want her to do."

"I see," said Bonnie. She was scratching her braces.

"I'm practicing psychology on worms so I can use psychology on her."

Bonnie bent for a closer look at one of the worms. "Do you want your mother to go right or left?"

I grinned. "Neither. I want her to go around in circles."

8.

Arf in Orbit

I want to tell you — worms have a lousy sense of direction. After I dropped them in the mazes they either went to sleep or the ones that weren't too tired to move squirmed. Every which way, except straight ahead to the T. One guy even loop-dy-looped himself into a pretzel.

"Maybe they're turned around backwards and they can't smell the compost," said Bonnie. I had to admit she had a point there. I mean, who knows which end of a worm is the nose? So we ran all over the yard and turned the worms the other way, including the ones that were resting.

"Hey, straight ahead, guys." But nobody caught on. "Maybe they're lying on their smellers," I said to Bonnie. This time we ran all over the yard and flipped them, smeller side up.

No luck. The only worms crawling in a straight line were crawling into the grass. "Uh-oh. Sorry, Max." Bonnie smushed one trying to convince it to stay inside.

"Let's put more compost in," I said. We ran around and sprinkled more dead potato skins and leaves.

"This looks like next week's meatloaf," said Bonnie.

We both crouched beside a maze and waited. Nothing was happening. I couldn't understand it. It worked on TV. Maybe worms don't have smellers, I thought. I was beginning to lose faith in psychology. And in worms.

Then Dad came out in his T-shirt and shorts. He was going jogging. "Hey, what are you doing to my lawn?"

"Don't worry, Dad, we'll put it back." I held up a clump of sod.

"If it isn't dead first. Oh well. It'll give me an excuse not to mow. Better not let your mother in the back yard." He glanced around. "What's going on here, anyway?"

While Dad did his warm-up exercises, I explained about the TV program I had seen. I didn't mention *why* I wanted to learn psychology. "But the worms won't crawl straight," I complained.

"You know what I always say," Dad answered.

"What?"

"Never trust a crooked worm." (Groan.) When my father doesn't know the answer to something he tells BAD jokes. Dad trotted down the driveway.

"Oh no," shouted Bonnie. "The worms are leaving." I got there just in time to see the tail end of a worm slipping into the dirt. (I *think* it was the tail end.) My father was right. Never trust a crooked worm.

"Now what do we do?"

"I guess we wait to see if they find the compost," said Bonnie.

While we waited for a worm (*any* worm: it could have tunneled here from China — I didn't care) to peep *up* from his pile of compost, Arf found us and was trotting around the yard peeping *down* all the worm holes. Which I can guarantee you wasn't helping the worms decide to come out. Would you come out if you were being stared at by an eye twice your size?

"Jeff wants you, Arf. Go find Jeff."

"No, don't chase him away," said Bonnie.

"He's scaring the worms."

"We don't *know* that."

"Sure we do."

"What evidence do you have?"

"You don't see any worms, do you?"

Bonnie went into her lawyer pose — stiff neck, hands behind her back. "We only know that the worms aren't reappearing and that Arf is sniffing the mazes. The connection may be purely accidental. We have to have evidence — EVIDENCE — to show a relationship between the two events." Bonnie's big on evidence. "What if we don't see any

worms because they're all going the other way — to
Mrs. Aiello's yard? As your attorney, I suggest we
practice on Arf. At least we know which end is the
nose."

Good ol' Bonnie. What a lawyer.

As soon as we tried to catch Arf, he took off, of
course, into Mrs. Aiello's yard. Everything was going to Mrs. Aiello's: worms *and* dogs.

Bonnie held the back door and I chased Arf to our
yard. Once he noticed the opening he galloped inside. We found him hiding under Jeff's bed, head-in,
in the farthest corner so he couldn't see us. (Smart
dog.)

"Come on, Arf. Come here." I used my sweetest
doggie voice. Arf's tail thumped twice and drooped.
I know that droopy-tail look. We'd have to drag
him out.

"This is a job for psychology," I said. The first
thing we needed was something Arf liked to eat.
Actually, if you took one look at Arf you'd know he
will eat anything. He's so round he looks like a bar-
rel running on four cigar stubs. I rummaged in the
kitchen for Doggie Donuts. There were a few left
in the box.

Bonnie and I slithered under Jeff's bed on our
elbows. "Here pooch-y. Here pooch-y." Arf turned
and looked over his shoulder.

"Quick, give me a Doggie Donut."

Bonnie handed me one and I fed it to Arf before

he turned his head away. Arf's tail wagged. "Food, Arf." He turned around under the bed so his mouth would be closer. I gave him another Doggie Donut and began backing out. He was coming out with me.

"Unfh." That was Bonnie's voice.

"Ow!" That was Jeff's voice.

"What are you doing under the bed?" I yelled at Jeff.

"I wanted to see what you were doing under the bed."

"I'm getting Arf out."

"Oh."

"Back up."

"Okay." Jeff pretended he was a train and tooted several times, then threw his engine into reverse. "CHUG-a chug-a, CHUG-a chug-a. WOOO-OOO." Then Bonnie backed up.

"Hurry up, Jeff." It was a slow train.

Jeff did a tour of the room. "CHUG-a chug-a, CHUG-a, chug-a." Arf the caboose was still hiding. Only his nose poked from beneath the bedspread. (That way he wouldn't miss any Doggie Donuts chug-chugging by.)

I reached for a Doggie Donut, but Jeff was munching the last one. "Jeff! Now what will I use to train Arf?"

"You can use Puff'ems," said Bonnie.

This is great, I thought. Kid eats dog food, dog eats kid food.

The Puff'ems were gone, too. Bonnie poked around in the pantry. "Hmm, does Arf like cookies?"

"Are you kidding?"

"We'll have to brush his teeth afterward."

"Mom will kill you," said Jeff.

"Not if she doesn't know they're gone," said Bonnie. "We'll buy more at Mr. Connelly's. My mom has a charge account."

"Right," I said a little uncertainly. I had a queer feeling this could mean trouble.

Fourteen boxes later Arf was trained. That was three boxes from our house, two from Bonnie's, and nineteen from Mr. Connelly's to make up for the ones we snitched. Mr. Connelly scratched his bald head and asked if we were *sure* Mrs. Silver wanted all these cookies. "Isn't your mother the dentist?"

"She's having a party." Bonnie smiled. "For all her patients."

The chocolate chippers were Arf's favorites. He would run out from under the bed, turn a clockwise circle, followed by a counterclockwise circle, and then he'd duck under Jeff's bed, ready to do it again.

I was doing cartwheels I was so happy.

There was just one itsy-bitsy problem. Arf wouldn't go around in circles unless he hid under the bed first. So we tried taking him down to the basement. Out of sight, out of mind, Grandpa says.

Usually Grandpa is right, but this time he messed up, because as soon as one of us, Bonnie or Jeff or I, showed Arf a chocolate chipper, Arf sprinted up both flights of stairs as fast as his cigar stubs would carry him, dived under Jeff's bed, screeched to a halt before he hit the wall, skittered back out, flung himself in a clockwise circle, flung himself in a counterclockwise circle, then collapsed under the bedspread, with his tongue stretched far enough past the fringe to collect his cookie.

I was so tired after the fourth trip up two flights of stairs I thought I was going to pant for the rest of my life. "There has to be a better — way, Bonnie." Bonnie was a trembling heap at the top of the stairs.

"We could — close Jeff's — door."

I didn't have enough air to answer. I just nodded and gave Arf his cookie. Then I led him out and closed Jeff's door.

"I'm staying — here — in case," said Bonnie.

"Pessimist."

"Lawyers — pessimists. Good for business. What kind of lawyer would I be — if I didn't believe in pain and suffering — and bankruptcy?"

Arf and I trudged to the basement. Slowly, carefully, I slipped a chocolate chipper from the box. "Please, Arf, do your dance here. Not in Jeff's room." I raised the cookie. All four stubs skidded across the linoleum and charged up the stairs.

Arf smacked nose-first into Jeff's door. He was whining in the hallway when I finally made it up.

"I think Arf wants his cookie," said Bonnie.

Karen had opened her door. "Would you mind? I have company." I could hear Fawn giggling. You call that company?

Just then Arf bolted past Karen into the room. He ducked under her bed and back out, spun two circles, one clockwise, one counterclockwise, then ducked under my bed.

"Get that filthy hound out of here!" Karen bellowed.

Arf wouldn't budge until I gave him his cookie.

"What a dip dog. He sure is bonzo." That was Fawn. Creep. I hoped she'd wake up some day with a first class case of head lice. I hoped she'd be so infested they'd creep down her forehead and into her eyebrows. Creep.

We went down to the basement to try again. This time I told Jeff to hang on to Arf's collar.

Arf dragged Jeff up the basement steps. About halfway up Jeff let go. I counted, "One thousand-one, one thousand-two, one thousand-three —"

"GET THAT ANIMAL OUT OF HERE!!" Karen sure can shout when she wants to. I guess she learned that in cheerleading. I coaxed Arf down with another cookie.

"Maybe Arf's had enough cookies," said Bonnie, scraping the filling from an Oreo. "I think we ought to practice tomorrow."

I agreed. Psychology is exhausting.

9.

Apologies

Bonnie, Jeff, and I were settled down for a nice peaceful game of three-handed War. Arf was sleeping on the couch, clawing the air every once in a while as if he were running up the stairs, when Mom returned from her shopping trip. She poked her head into the family room. "Hi."

I made a point of letting Jeff's card beat my card. "Usually, the king beats the six, Jeff, but since you're new at this — War's a tough game to learn — I'll let you take my king. Only this time, though."

Jeff shuffled his pile, spilling most of it. "I'm winning. See all my cards?" He held them up for Mom.

"Has sister been playing with you today?"

"We played train and we played Ring Around the Rosie with Arf," said Jeff.

"How nice."

A few minutes later Mom was carrying a plate of chocolate chippers into the family room. She called for Karen and Fawn to join us. "Don't think you're off the hook. You're on good behavior," she muttered my way. "Help yourself, children."

No sooner had she set the dish on the coffee table than Arf woke up from a sound sleep, his nostrils flared like bugles.

One whiff and he tore down to the basement, up the stairs into Karen's room ("GET OUT OF HERE!"), Jeff's room (Whap!), back to the family room, did two circles around the rug, one clockwise, one counterclockwise, flopped under the coffee table, and wouldn't stop whining until I sneaked him a cookie.

"My goodness. What's gotten into Arf?" asked Mom.

"A lot of cookies," said Jeff. I shoved a cookie in Jeff's mouth before he could say more.

Arf must have seen me because he did it again. He streaked down to the basement and halfway upstairs. Karen and Fawn shrieked when he ran into them; Arf thought he'd hit Jeff's door again. He turned around, raced down to the family room to the coffee table, where he whirled — and fainted.

At least it looked as if he had fainted. He lay flat on his back like a corpse with his paws pointing straight up. But I knew better. His tongue was waiting for a cookie.

Mom stared. Karen stared. Fawn nearly popped her contact lenses. I jumped to the floor. Last year Patty Ryan's mother taught us artificial respiration in Scouts. I never thought I'd be using it on Arf.

"Arf's had a hard day, that's all," I said, pumping his legs. "I put him on a physical fitness plan. Running up and down stairs is supposed to be good for you. Builds a strong heart and lungs. Like Dad. What he needs now is bed rest. I think I'll sing him a lullabye or two, or three." I grabbed a handful of cookies. "You don't mind if I finish mine while I put Arf to bed, do you?"

"Are you sure he's all right?" asked Mom. Her eyebrows knit together in a big question mark. "He certainly is acting peculiar."

"When isn't Arf peculiar?" said Karen. "Pets act like their masters."

I wiggled my ears at my sister. "Ha ha, Karen. Very witty. No wonder your gerbil was so smelly before it died."

I had to cover Arf's eyes as I led him to his basket in the laundry room. Arf gobbled down the chocolate chippers, while I sat on the floor next to the dryer and sang a couple of nursery rhymes. Pretty soon he was snoring.

This was terrible. Every time someone opened a box of cookies, Arf was going to crash through the house like a drunken bus. And he'd keep adding stops. In a few days he'd be running under every bed and table in town. What had I done to him? A dog can't go through life blindfolded.

I shuddered. What would psychology do to my

mother? How would I explain it to my father, or Jeff, when she started crawling under tables and begging for cookies? I wanted to tell Mrs. Silver. I was never using psychology again. I mean, I was scared of the stuff.

That night I tossed and turned. I kept seeing Arf and my mother. They were miserable. They both had tooth decay and needed quadruple by-pass stomach surgery.

I'd have to reform. It was the only way to get any sleep. I tiptoed over to Karen's bed and apologized for the painted monster choppers and for sparkling my teeth at her in the middle of the night. I turned down the bathroom scales another two pounds. That was for my mother. Then I sneaked into Jeff's room and apologized to Arf under the bed. Poor Arf.

On second thought, before I climbed under the covers again, I stood next to Queen Karen and took back my apology. She deserved more than green teeth.

10.

Congratulations, Ms. Goode

The next day Mom showed me the shoes she had bought when she went shopping. "They're sensible shoes for Girl Scouts," Mom said proudly. They were flat rubber-soled ones, the kind Miss Halibut wears.

"Well?" asked Mom.

"I guess I'm not used to seeing you looking so sensible — er — so short. Do you suppose there's such a thing as sensible high heels?"

This is serious, I said to myself. Urgent, I said to myself. Mom wasn't the kind of mother to trade in her spikes lightly. If we wanted to get her out of Girl Scouts, Bonnie and I needed to come up with something fast. Noise hadn't worked. I didn't dare try psychology. What else was left?

I called Bonnie. "Things are bad. Really bad." I told her about the shoes.

"She bought *one* pair of sensible shoes. In a couple of months she'll decide she can't stand them and she'll throw them away."

"Bonnie, you don't understand. They're green. To match her uniform."

Bonnie was quiet. "You're right. This is serious. I'd even say urgent. Can you come over for a consultation?"

"I have to play with Jeff first. I'm still on probation with my mom."

"Come as soon as you can. Over."

Jeff and I played dinosaur for a while, then I told him I had to go to the bathroom. I turned on the walkie-talkie for him before I left. With that thing to play with he'd never miss me.

I took the shortcut through the hedge to Bonnie's. Bonnie was watching *People's Court.* I never interrupt her during *People's Court.* I made myself comfortable in the pillows, while Bonnie took notes on her legal pad.

Legal paper is long and yellow. Bonnie uses it for her file of cases. She says they're her precedents. (I used to think they were presidents, but they're not.)

Every lawyer has a stack of precedents. Those are the cases he knows about and he uses them to argue So-and-So did this or that. I think Bonnie figures if she starts collecting them now she'll have more than anybody else and she'll win.

"A fascinating case," said Bonnie, turning off the TV. She gestured at the blank screen with her pencil. "This guy, he's the party of the first part. He's suing the party of the second part."

"Which one was he?"

Bonnie pointed to the right of the blank screen. "This one."

"Oh, I see," I said, which was a lot of baloney because I couldn't see a thing.

"He's suing for lost property value."

"Huh? How did he lose it?"

"He hasn't lost it yet. But he will if he tries to sell his house, because the party of the second part painted his house lime green with pink trim. The party of the first part and the party of the second part live next door to each other. And the party of the first part says he can't stand to look out his window anymore.

"The party of the first part says the party of the second part did it to get even with the party of the first part because the party of the first part put up a chain-link fence, which the party of the second part said was an insult, which the party of the first part said was his right, so the party of the second part—"

Bonnie's pencil was flying so fast from the left to right and right to left that I was too dizzy to hear about all those parties who weren't really there anyway. At last her pencil stopped. "So who won?" I asked.

"Nobody did. Case dismissed. Technically, the damage hadn't occurred yet, since the guy hadn't tried to sell his house." Bonnie's grin widened to her ears. "However, the judge did suggest to the party of the first part that he paint his house — uh — an interesting color, too." Bonnie made an elaborate wink.

She pulled out her legal pad and wrote with a flourish: "Case No. 134. Legal precedent: If you can't beat 'em, join 'em."

"I think this very precedent could be most helpful in your case," said Bonnie. She crossed one leg over the other and studied her jiggling toe. I watched, too, hoping I'd see something, but Bonnie's toe was as blank as the TV screen.

"I'm already joined. I'm trying to un-join," I said.

"That's the point. You've been trying to beat them and it hasn't worked."

"You can say that again."

Bonnie said it again. "It hasn't worked."

"Do you have to rub it in? I'm your best client, Bonnie," I warned. "Who else do you know who has as many cases as I do?"

Bonnie looked ashamed for about two seconds. She hunched over her yellow sheets, underlined a few sentences, then stabbed the eraser end of her pencil at me. "If he paints his house lime green and pink, you paint yours purple and orange. If your mother joins the Girl Scouts, you —"

"Join the circus?" I said.

Bonnie threw her hand to her forehead and made a disgusted face beneath the shower of yellow papers.

"I'm the *only* client you've got, Bonnie," I reminded her. I was running out of patience. I wanted answers, not a game-show quiz.

Bonnie turned to the television set again. "The party of the second part paints his house green and pink. So the party of the first part paints his house with zebra stripes."

"Yucch."

"Right. Now what's going to happen?"

"Maybe this guy" — I touched the screen — "will paint his back a regular color" — I touched again — "if the other guy does."

"Right! You've got it!"

"*What* have I got?"

"Okay, tell me what we usually do in Girl Scouts. We sell cookies, we —"

"We tie knots, we go camping. Sometimes we make candles. Once we had a car wash —" Suddenly I knew what Bonnie was trying to get me to see. It was so exciting *I* threw Bonnie's papers. "My mother joins Girl Scouts, I turn into Superscout!"

Bonnie leaped up and pumped my hand so hard I felt like the lever on one of Grandpa's gambling machines in Atlantic City. "That's it! Congratulations, Ms. Goode. Congratulations!"

This time we were going to get to Mom. I knew it down to my sneakers.

11.

Superscout

Mom gagged on her coffee the next day when she saw me wearing my Girl Scout uniform. "Our troop meeting is *tomorrow*, Maxine."

"I know," I said, smiling politely. (At least I think it was polite. It had been a while.) "I just wanted to wear it." Mom got excited and fluttery. I knew what she was thinking — that I had changed my mind about Scouts, and maybe about Ruth Ellen.

All day in school I felt like a jerk. I can't stand skirts, and the badge sash covered up the best part of my Mean Maxine shirt. On top of that Patty Ryan asked me thirty thousand times why I was wearing it. I told her I was planning to sell Girl Scout cookies after school. I thought that would shut her up. No such luck.

"What for? The sale doesn't start until next week."

"So I can have my name in the *Guinness Book of World Records*. For selling the most Girl Scout cookies. What else?"

"Gee," said Patty, "I didn't know they had that in the *Guinness Book of Records.*" She looked as if she might consider trying for the record, too.

"Oh, sure. They have everything in there." If it wasn't it ought to be. After all, they have things like the most people in a telephone booth and the most goldfish swallowed. Why not the most Girl Scout cookies sold?

During recess word spread that I was already selling cookies. As we were lining up to go back inside, Ruth Ellen squeezed ahead of me. "How many boxes have you sold, toad?"

Obviously I hadn't sold any cookies yet, but I wasn't about to admit that to Ruth Ellen. "Ohh, just a few — er — quite a few."

"How many?"

"Quite a few — dozen I meant."

"How many is quite a few dozen?"

"What's it to you?" I said, stalling.

"Two dozen? Five? Ten?"

"More than that," I lied. "Twice as much. Twenty dozen."

"Ha. I beat you. I sold two hundred and sixty-three boxes last year."

(I was amazed she could count that high.)

"Oh, this is just from the people on my block. I haven't tried a lot of the places I have in mind yet."

First Ruth Ellen gasped. Then she scowled. The

way she marched inside I knew this wasn't the end of it.

By the time our Girl Scout meeting rolled around, I had sold more cookies than I ever dreamed of selling, or at least everybody thought I had. Patty told her mother, Mrs. Ryan told Mrs. Wolfe, Mrs. Wolfe mentioned to Mom how happy she must be, since she was the one in charge of the cookie sale — and Mom grilled me. "Did you *really* sell four hundred and forty boxes of cookies?"

Four hundred and forty boxes? I gulped. How do you tell your mother it was only a teensy lie when it started? I didn't know, so I told another teensy lie. "Sure, Mom."

I guess she wanted to believe me because on Tuesday, Mrs. Wolfe announced I had sold four hundred and *fifty* boxes and urged the other girls to follow my excellent example. "I think Maxine deserves a big, big Girl Scout thank you."

The girls broke into a loud cheer — all except Ruth Ellen and darling Darlene.

My mother glowed. GLOWED. Like a light blub. Proud of *me*, Maxine No-Goode Goode? The last time I could remember my mother being proud of me was when I learned how to tie my shoe laces.

"Hey, Max." Bonnie tugged at my sash. "When did you sell all those cookies?"

"Shhh," I whispered. "Tell you later."

"Man-o-man, are you in trouble," Bonnie said when I explained. "If this were going to trial, I wouldn't touch it." I gave Bonnie a cross look. "Okay, okay. You'd better start selling cookies — pronto — before someone asks to see the orders."

"Superscout was your idea, remember?"

Bonnie answered cautiously. "Yeah."

"Then *we* had better start selling cookies. Pronto. Two hundred and twenty-five boxes for you. Two hundred twenty-five for me." I punched Bonnie on the arm. "Right, pal?"

"I was afraid you'd say that."

I went to Grandpa's first. When I told him how many boxes I had to sell, he upped his order from last year's and offered to go with me to the Senior Citizens'. He said it was about time he got even for all those potholders he had had to buy.

On Wednesday I went to Mr. Connelly's Corner Store. He let me stand next to the cold cuts. He thought it was good for business to let customers know he was public-minded and a Girl Scout booster. Mr. Connelly did seem a smidge annoyed though, when Mrs. DeVore bought my cookies instead of her usual deli platter for her Save-the-Water-Street Bridge Club meeting.

I stopped by Bonnie's house afterward to see how she was doing selling cookies.

"Fifteen boxes," said Bonnie. "To myself."

"Maybe you don't have the right technique, Bonnie. You have to stare at them and make them feel guilty. That's what I do."

"Patty Ryan says Ruth Ellen is bragging that she's selling tons of cookies where her father works. No one dares to turn her down because her father's the new boss. And he promised her a private line for her teen phone, if she sells five hundred boxes."

"That's fifty more than me," I screeched. Bonnie nodded wearily. I fumed.

That settled it. I was going for broke. I was going to sell so many cookies that Ruth Ellen would never catch up. There was only room for one Superscout in Troop 914. Me.

Dad was visiting a client that afternoon, so I had the corporation all to myself. I hopped into his swivel chair and twirled around a few times to move the seat up, then I pulled the phone and his customer file closer.

Might as well start with the A's. I punched the buttons. Beep. Beep. Boop. Beep. Beep. Boop. Beep. This beat going door-to-door.

"Hello, Adam and Eve's Health Club. Miss Flossy speaking. No body job is too big. If you starve it, we'll rebuild it. Our special bargain this week — bring a friend and you get a month free."

"I'd love to, Miss Flossy, but Goode Associates, Incorporated, is donating its telephone line and office space for Girl Scout Troop Number 914 to sell Girl Scout cookies, and I wondered —"

"Cookies?"

"Yes, we're selling chocolate cremes, vanilla cremes, peanut-butter jumbles, and chocolate thin mints."

"Thin? Adam and Eve's has a weight reduction warranty, a one time special only —"

"But I'm not calling about weight reduction. I'm calling because —"

"It's never too soon to begin weight consciousness-raising. Let me send you information about our ninety-day introductory offer."

I talked louder. "I'd like to get my name in the *Guinness Book of Records.*"

"At Adam and Eve's you lose unsightly pounds in record time. Set a record at our —"

"*Miss Flossy!!*" I screamed. There was a delicate silence at the other end. "Miss Flossy, you're probably on commission, right?" I knew all about commissions from my dad. They were always too little money for the work.

"How did you guess?"

"I'm trying to sell Girl Scout cookies —"

"Oh, are you on commission, too?"

"No!" I shouted. "Look, I'm selling cookies and you're selling memberships to your health club. Maybe we could get together on this. You scratch my back, I'll scratch yours." (That was another one of Bonnie's precedents from *People's Court*; a woman sued her landlord because her apartment was hopping with fleas.)

"Oh," Miss Flossy chirped, "we have a wonderful magic-hands machine designed specially to gently scratch and massage —"

I couldn't stand it anymore. I growled. It was my Mean Maxine growl. Miss Flossy stopped.

"Miss Flossy, I can help you."

"You can?"

"Yes, Miss Flossy. I'm promoting junk food. You should be, too. If you bought a lot of Girl Scout cookies and gave them away free you'd have more customers who needed their bodies rebuilt. Get the picture?"

"Oh-h-h, I do-o see." Miss Flossy sounded as if someone had just switched the lights on. "And, of course, it's to help the Girl Scouts. You're a mighty clever little girl, Miss — Miss —"

"Maxine Goode. Jerry Goode's daughter from Goode Associates, Incorporated."

"How many cookies is that you have?"

"As many as you want. How about two hundred boxes?"

"I'll take three hundred."

"Is that three hundred of each kind, or altogether?" I asked.

Miss Flossy giggled. "You Girl Scouts drive a hard bargain."

I sold twenty-two hundred boxes of Girl Scout cookies. Adam and Eve's Health Spa ordered most of them. A vacuum cleaner salesman on Dad's list bought a bunch more. (He used to sell computers, too, he said.) He bought cookies to pass out to people when he made calls. (That was my idea. He really liked it and told me to contact him when I was grown up; maybe we could do more business together.)

Mr. Lee at China Chopsticks Eat-In or Carry-Out ordered several cartons to use as fortune cookies. He said he was going to tape the fortunes to the bottoms of the cookies. The firefighters at the firehouse bought vanilla and chocolate cremes because they're always losing their checker pieces when they rush out to fires, and a police officer in the station house next door bought a couple of boxes of peanut-butter jumbles to tide over lost children until their families phoned.

That was only the beginning of my Superscout campaign. When I wasn't selling Girl Scout cookies I was tying knots. I tied everything that had two ends — the sleeves on my turtleneck, bed sheets. I borrowed Dad's ties to make square knots. I lassoed Jeff to his breakfast chair with two half hitches, which Karen thought was pretty funny, until she tried to put on her brand new Sergio Egg-plant-ay jeans. (Two overhand knots.)

(Populars have no sense of humor.)

But the clincher was my Girl Scout uniform. I wore it every day.

The first couple of days Mom seemed glad to wash and iron it. Then for a couple of days she thought it was amusing. By Friday morning I could tell she wanted to rip something to shreds — either me or the uniform. "Do you have to, Maxine?"

"I need it to sell cookies. I'm going to be in the *Guinness Book of Records*."

"This is ridiculous," Mom muttered. I pretended not to hear.

Queen Karen pointed at my outfit. "Good grief! Four days in that?"

"*Five*," said Mom.

"How gross. She *must* be ill. I hope it isn't catching."

The way Mom looked you knew it was catching.

I wore my uniform all weekend, too.

12.

Vultures over Dead Meat

Miss Flossy called one day while I was at school. Mom took the call. Miss Flossy wanted to change her order to mostly thin mints. She thought thin mints might be better for the health spa's image.

Mom was waiting for me at the door when I came home. Her red nail polish was ragged and jittery-looking; she had been chewing her fingers. Shiny, smooth nails mean all's clear. Anything else means look out! I was heading for cover, but those pesky fingernails reached over and grabbed me by the book bag.

"What's this about twelve hundred boxes of Girl Scout cookies for the Garden of Eden?"

"It's called Adam and Eve's," I said squirming, "and it's a health spa, not the Garden of Eden." (It's very hard to escape when you are suspended by your book bag. Your arms turn into wings.)

"The cookies, Maxine," Mom squeaked. "Tell me about the cookies. Tell me we won't have to deliver twelve hundred boxes."

"We won't have to deliver twelve hundred boxes," I replied, flapping.

"Whew. With a name like Miss Flossy I had a hunch that lady was a kook." She dropped the book bag. "Can you imagine what the Girl Scout Council would have said? Twelve hundred boxes—"

Mom thought about twelve hundred boxes of Girl Scout cookies. She looked as if the outer-space brain snatchers were after her. You could just see her brain cells overload and frizz. "Why, they would be so—so overwhelmed—and so proud," she said, surprised at her own idea.

Well, if she felt that way about it. "Actually, it's twenty-two hundred and three boxes. Altogether," I said, brushing off my kneepads.

That's when my mother's eyes bulged like tennis balls. "Not twelve hundred? Twenty-two hundred and three? Altogether? I see. Altogether." She staggered and tripped over a bread crumb on her way to the floor.

"Mom? Are you okay? You aren't going to sue, are you?"

She stared at the ceiling. "If I can manage four hundred and fifty"—she said, gulping air like a fish—"why not a couple of thousand more?" (Glub Glub.) Then Mom giggled.

Half an hour later Mom was still staring at the ceiling and giggling. I looked up. There was the ceiling, and, if you looked close, a few strands of cobwebs from the ceiling to the light fixture. I had to admit after you stared at them for a *long* time the cobwebs were somewhat funny — not a riot exactly, but worth a few *hardy har har's*.

I went to my room to think about it, when Bonnie called on the walkie-talkie. Bonnie was making strange noises. I thought at first it was her yawn. Bonnie has a weird yawn. That's something I try not to mention, especially since yawns are kind of strange anyway, if you know what I mean, with that thing like a dangly earring hanging in the back of your throat.

But it was just Bonnie feeling sorry for herself. This was minestrone soup week at the Silvers' house. "I hate zucchini," she grumbled, "and by Friday I think I may hate chickpeas. If you come over, you can have mine."

"No thanks. I'm Superscout, remember? A Superscout cleans her plate at dinner. I just hope my mom makes something I can stand. Besides, I wouldn't want you to run out."

"That's why I invited you. I was hoping we would."

"Hey, I think it's working, Bonnie."

"What's working?"

"You know, 'If you can't beat 'em, join 'em.' Yesterday she *begged* me to wear my blue jeans and my baseball cap. And today she went hysterical." I told Bonnie about the Girl Scout cookies. All two thousand, two hundred, and three boxes of them. I was trying to calculate how many cookies that was. When it came to more than twenty thousand, Bonnie started making strange noises again. Must be the zucchini getting to her, I thought.

Bonnie stammered, "Isn't that—a lot of—cookies?"

"That's the idea. I'd sell more if I could find customers. I was wondering about your mother's patient list—"

"No! Don't!—don't sell any more cookies."

I didn't know minestrone soup made people so nervous. "Why not?"

"There's something very important I need to discuss with you first."

"Is this a legal matter?" Bonnie didn't answer. I whistled. "Hi-yo, Silver."

Finally Bonnie's brain clanked into place. "I read your horror-scope for this month and you'd better go into deep freeze for a while. It was *terrible*." (Reading my horror-scope is a fringe benefit Bonnie gives for free. I'm very superstitious. When you have as much crummy luck as I do, you become superstitious.)

"What did it say?"

"You don't want to know."

"That bad?"

"It said an old problem would reappear and circle like vultures over dead meat."

"Vultures! Dead meat!" I quivered. "Is there any way to stop it?"

I could hear Bonnie tapping her braces. "No."

"I'd better check on my mother, Bonnie. Over."

Mom was fixing dinner. It was even something I could eat, beef stew. Dead meat, for sure, but this couldn't be it. Vultures didn't giggle as far as I knew.

Mom did another nosedive a few days later when we handed in our cookie orders. Ruth Ellen had sold exactly five hundred boxes (and she let everyone know she was now the stuck-up owner of a teen phone *with* a private line). Patty Ryan sold two hundred thirty plus boxes. Jennifer sold ninety-nine. (Bonnie still had fifteen.)

After Mom added them all and did her nosedive and Mrs. Wolfe helped her up, Mom said when she fell she had been thinking about where to store all those cookies when they came and she had had this irresistible urge to grab a book bag and wring it by the neck.

Mrs. Wolfe didn't know what Mom was talking about, but I sure did.

I spent a lot of time after that in the corporation closet. Dad kept checking on me and asking me about my eyes and would I like to talk things over with Dr. Schmaltz. I told him I was working on a science project for school and every time he opened the door he ruined it. He finally left me alone.

Nothing happened — any worse than usual, that is. I told Dad I got an A and came out of the closet. Bonnie must have read my horror-scope wrong.

But horror-scopes have a way of coming true when you least expect it.

Late one afternoon when I was babysitting Jeff, Norman our mail carrier rang the doorbell. He had a package for us. "I have more for you out in the truck," said Norman, "but they're under other boxes. I'll be back later."

"Okay, Norman," I said closing the door. That was strange. Why would Norman have more for us? I tried to guess what was inside. As soon as I shook the package, I knew what it was.

So did Arf. Unfortunately.

Before I could finish opening the carton, Arf had zoomed all over the house in circles, then dropped panting at my feet. When I didn't give him his cookie, he did it again. And again. And again.

I got motion sickness just watching him. What could I do? We needed every box. Unopened.

Doggie Donuts slowed Arf down, but as soon as we ran out of Donuts he turned back into a boomerang. I managed to find one stale store-bought cookie in my book bag. It had lost its cookie smell so long ago that Arf thought it was a hockey puck and slapped it into the garbage can.

Then the doorbell rang. I peeked through the glass curtains. It was Norman. He was back with another package.

Dad was out of the office, so while Arf did part of his boomerang routine in the basement, I hustled upstairs and stashed both cartons of cookies in the corporation closet. Arf found me empty-handed, hiding under my dad's desk. He looked totally confused.

Until the doorbell rang. His ears and tail perked up.

"Oh, no, you don't! Jeff, don't open it!" I screamed, as Arf slipped out of the hammerlock I had on his right front paw.

Too late. Arf was chasing in mad circles around Norman. Norman twirled on our doorstep like a ballerina.

Jeff and I dived for Arf. Arf bolted for the yard, his back legs skidding and fish-tailing on the turns. Just when I thought I had him cornered, he sneaked past and did another dozen laps around Norman.

Norman was wobbling, about to topple. "Help. Help."

I ran upstairs. "Throw me the cookies," I yelled from the corporation window.

Norman glanced at the package he held over his

head. "This?" The way he threw it you would have thought Norman was getting rid of a hand grenade. No question what kind of cookies they were now — peanut-butter *crumbles*.

"Hey, Norman, stay in the mail truck and honk your horn next time. I'll come out and get it," I hollered as he ran down the sidewalk.

Norman didn't look back. "Sure thing, Maxine. I'd be happy to stay in the truck." He jumped into his waiting vehicle. "How about if I stay at the post office and honk? Better yet, I'll stay home and honk."

After school the next day Mom's hello had that what-did-you-do-now? tone. I tried to play it cool but inside I knew I wasn't cool. I was dead meat and the vultures were closing in.

"The postmaster called today, dear. He said Norman won't deliver the mail unless we can guarantee him safe passage to the curb. Did something happen yesterday while I was out, dear?" Mom tapped her fingers on her elbow. Drumrolls on her elbow means she expects an answer.

"Gee, Mom, not a thing," I said and charged up the stairs before she could wring my book bag by the neck.

I huddled over the walkie-talkie. "Maxine to Masked Man. Come in. May Day! May Day!"

"You don't have to shout," Bonnie answered.

"Bonnie, I met the vulture."

(Astonishment.) "You did?"

"Yeah. It's my mother."

"I told you it was bad."

Bonnie and I held a consultation over the walkie-talkies. Bonnie is very imaginative. She suggested I rig a basket and pulley system for hauling the packages up to the second floor. "That way you won't have to open the door," said Bonnie, "and Norman won't have to run to his truck."

Norman and I worked out a signal so I'd know he'd made a delivery. He honked a bicycle horn, which was attached to the pulley rope, and I'd pull it up. Norman was very happy with the arrangement. Mom was semi-happy with the arrangement. Jeff tried to take a ride in it.

Bonnie's fee for her advice was that I get her out of her minestrone bind. That was simple enough. The next time Mrs. Silver made minestrone I slipped a tin of red pepper into the soup while she was reheating it. She had to take Bonnie to Burger Heaven for dinner. Mrs. Silver never made minestrone again.

13.

Cookie Special Delivery

There were Girl Scout cookies everywhere: in the kitchen, down in the basement, in a corner of the living room, under our beds, in Dad's office, even in Arf's doghouse.

I thought for sure Arf would turn into a merry-go-round, but he was too exhausted to care anymore. The last load of boxes came through the corporation window and he tried to hide under his water dish.

Do you know what three thousand plus boxes of Girl Scout cookies *smell* like? Peanut butter. We were buried in it. For some reason the peanut-butter jumbles smelled the most.

I borrowed Bonnie's snorkel and face mask, so I didn't mind too much. Of course Queen Karen would make a big deal out of it. Her clothes smelled. What would her friends think? Yakity yakity.

"Just tell them it's peanut-butter perfume," I said. She didn't go for that idea.

By then my father had found out from a few of his clients that I had used his customer list to sell cookies. I told him Mr. Connelly said it was good for business. He made me promise if I had any more business suggestions I would speak to him first. In the meantime, the corporation was off-limits. Not that I could get in anyway — with all those cookies.

Saturday morning Mom and I set out early to make deliveries. I wore my Girl Scout uniform, my kneepads, and my basketball hightops. I dressed up because Dad said I'd better make a good impression, to protect his business interests.

We delivered cookies to the girls in the troop first. That took most of the morning. "Only twenty-two hundred more to go," Mom sang after we had unloaded the last girl's cookies. She was trying real hard to make it seem as though delivering Girl Scout cookies was the most fun she'd had in years, but I knew better. Mom was singing because her jaw was clenched too tight to talk.

"Twenty-two hundred and three," I sang back.

"Which way to the Garden of Eden?" she sang.

"Adam and Eve's," I sang.

Miss Flossy didn't look at all the way I expected — you know, the health spa type. She was more the butcher shop type — round and beefy. In fact, she reminded me of Mean Maxine.

She wouldn't let us leave without a tour of Adam and Eve's.

"I suppose that's the least we can do for our best customer," Mom sang under her breath. (She was starting to sound just a bit out of tune.)

"Our special this week is the extended family plan," Miss Flossy gabbed, demonstrating the rowing machine. "That includes cousins and grandparents."

"How about fat dogs?"

Miss Flossy grinned. "That's the immediate family plan."

Then we were rounding the corner from the locker room to the weight training room and on the opposite wall, bigger than real life, was a poster of Mean Maxine lifting barbells. It took my breath away.

I had thought health spas were for people who wanted to look like cheerleaders. I didn't know a health spa could make you look like Mean Maxine.

Mom caught one glimpse of the poster, grabbed my hand, said, "Oh, no, you don't!" and ran out of the building, dragging me behind her.

Sniff.

After the health spa, we visited the vacuum cleaner salesman. He didn't seem to care what kind of cookies we had for him, as long as they looked messy when he stomped them into a rug and as long as they came up in his Deluxe Flex-O-Matic Scurf 'n' Turf vacuum cleaner.

Mr. Klunkermeyer — that was his name — was very entertaining. He tapdanced and played "New York, New York" on the nozzle of his dust wand.

"Just giving people more for their vacuuming dollar," he said. He said you have to be entertaining these days or people won't buy. I think he was hoping to sell a Deluxe Flex-O-Matic Scurf 'n' Turf cleaner to my mother. He offered her a free, no-obligation, strictly-a-demonstration at our house.

"If you try the Deluxe Flex-O-Matic Scurf 'n' Turf vacuum cleaner for ten days I'll throw in the scented vacuum cleaner bags," said Mr. Klunkermeyer. "Lemon, Mint, or Raspberry-Rhubarb!" Mr. Klunkermeyer bent closer to Mom so that they were eyeball-to-eyeball. "Raspberry-Rhubarb is especially nice. Makes your whole house smell like fresh-baked pie."

I explained to Mr. Klunkermeyer that Mom doesn't vacuum anymore because she's Doing Something. (Mom tried to kick me in the shins, but, luckily, my kneepads had slipped.)

Mr. Klunkermeyer sighed. "What can you do? It's a dying business."

"If anybody else dares to try to sell me one more thing," snarled Mom, as we left, "I'm going to declare bankruptcy."

"I know a cheap lawyer," I offered. Mom's eyes narrowed to teeny slits. I think she never wanted to see me again. I decided I'd better disappear under the cookies at the back of the station wagon.

Our next stop was the firehouse. No one tried to

sell Mom anything, although by the time we were finished delivering the cookies she may have wished they had.

Not that the firefighters were unfriendly. They were very friendly. They were so friendly that they offered to let us climb up in their brand-new fire engine, which was not red, by the way. It was a light pea-soup color. I think fire engines should be red — red for fires. Who ever heard of a fire the color of pea soup?

We snooped all over the truck while Chief Bunsen explained the various hoses and nozzles and pumps and ladders. The pumps were his favorite part. That was obvious. He really got excited when he talked about water pressure and gauges.

"Jeff would love this," Mom commented.

All of a sudden the station house was exploding with sound. Heavy coats and boots popped out of ceilings and lockers onto the truck beside us. The doors opened as if by magic. Someone started up the fire engine.

Mom and I looked at each other. "Guess we'll have to deliver cookies another day, Mom." Mom quickly climbed down off the truck. I backed down the ladder slowly, wondering what it was like to ride a fire engine to a fire, when the truck sprang forward. I slipped on the top rung.

The truck was nosing into the intersection of

Maple and Prospect, carrying me with it. More firefighters were jumping aboard. I waved my arms. "Hey, Mom, look!"

Mom looked as if she were choking on her Adam's apple. (Why do they call it an Adam's apple? After all, it was Eve's apple, wasn't it?) "Maxine B. Goode, you get off that truck. *Immediately!*"

Mom wasn't singing anymore. She was shouting. The jig was up.

I called to a firefighter. "Yoo-hoo. Yoo-hoo. This is my first ride on a fire engine. How do I get off?" I guess he didn't hear me. I tried again. "Yoo-hoo. Yoo-hoo. This is my stop." He still didn't hear me.

The engine was rumbling louder, signaling that it was about ready to pull away. It was now or never. I did a sideways swan jump over the rear end of the truck. Splat! I crash-landed in a pile of rubber hoses.

"It's about time," said Mom.

It didn't help that the fire was a false alarm. The engine went out and came right back. The rest of the day Mom did a slow burn; her nostrils would smoke every once in a while. Maybe after her scare she thought she deserved a real fire.

Mom wouldn't let me come in with her to deliver cookies to the police station, or to Mr. Lee's restaurant. "It's too risky," she said. "You'll end up in the middle of a robbery or in somebody's moo goo gai pan."

After the last box was handed over, Mom slumped in the driver's seat. She twiddled her thumbs for a long time. Either she was contemplating doing a little bodily harm to a certain Superscout, or she was going to quit. I decided it was bodily harm. The twiddling appeared to be sharpening her fingernails.

The only thing that could save me was the *Guinness Book of Records*. I was thinking of running out and buying a copy. To hold in front of my body.

Mom tapped her fingernails together. The tips glistened in the sun like steel blades. "Next year we're going to sell pickled pigs feet," said Mom. "Not even you could sell twenty-two hundred and three jars of pickled pigs feet." Then Mom grinned her crocodile grin.

"You have a point there, Mom," I said, staring at her teeth and her fingernails. "In fact, several."

14.

Red, White, and True Blue

Even after we sent the Girl Scout Council its share of the cookie money, our troop had a lot left over. Mrs. Wolfe called a meeting to decide what to do with it. "I think Maxine should suggest something first," said Mrs. Wolfe, "since she's responsible for this lovely state of affairs."

Ruth Ellen sat in the back snickering and talking too loud about her teen phone. She had been a total pain lately — getting darling Darlene and the other populars to call me Cookie and Fig Newton and giggling like an idiot when they did. I was so fed up I brought some of Arf's crunchies to school and sprinkled the crumbs in her gym suit. Miss Halibut made me stay after to clean up the locker room but it was worth it. For three days Ruth Ellen smelled like a bag of Fido.

If you ask me, she was jealous.

Mrs. Wolfe patted my baseball cap and beamed at Mom. Mom beamed back at us. Mom's beam was more like a pen light, though. Mrs. Wolfe's was a spotlight. In case you hadn't guessed, Mrs. Wolfe is a big smiler. She always smiles as though she's saying "cheese" for the camera. Grown-ups with cheese smiles are the only ones who appreciate children like me.

As I basked in Girl Scout glory, I was sorry I wasn't wearing my uniform. My uniform was so stiff by now it had walked itself to the washing machine.

I was trying to come up with a whopper of an idea for what to do with the money, but my mother was being very distracting. (She talks about *me* disturbing people.) She kept winking at me and tilting her head back. It made me think of gargling. Which wasn't much of an idea.

Then the light dawned. So *that's* why Mom had gotten us lost downtown yesterday! We were taking Jeff to the doctor's for a checkup. She did it on the way home, too. I thought there was something fishy. It's hard to get lost in a downtown four blocks wide that you've lived in for ten years. Especially twice.

Twice she had pulled into the same parking space beside the village square and had said, "Goodness, the old town hall certainly could use sprucing up. A new flag would be nice, don't you think, dear?"

"I like faded, raggedy flags," I said. (That's probably why we had to go back; I didn't take the hint the first time. The second time, Jeff said *he* liked faded, raggedy flags.)

Mom and Mrs. Wolfe must have cooked up this

scheme to let me suggest something, together. (Unfortunately, smilers are easily taken in by schemers.)

Now I knew what I wanted. It wasn't what my mother wanted. My mother wanted mé to suggest a worthwhile cause. Such as donating a new flag for the village square. I wanted to be selfish. I wanted to go camping at Lake Wocka Wocka. I squirmed, thinking of all I'd miss if I said Wocka Wocka.

As fast as I could, I said, "IthinkweshouldbuyanewflagforCampWockaWocka." I peeked. The walls didn't collapse. Glass didn't fly out of the windows.

"A flag for Wocka Wocka! What a splendid idea!" Mrs. Wolfe exclaimed. "Maxine, you're a genius."

(A genius? Can you guess how many times in my life I've been called a genius? I've been called lots of things, especially by Miss Halibut, and by the principal. They could go in the *Guinness Book of Records* for the things they know to call people. I've been shocking forty-two times, and outrageous thirteen times, but never a genius. For a minute I went crazy and swore I'd wear my Girl Scout uniform for the rest of my life.)

Mrs. Wolfe did this dance around the meeting room, making little excited claps with her hands. I think the dance was Spanish. "This could be our fall service project," she said. "Think of all the things that need improving at Wocka Wocka. There's the footbridge, the outhouses need painting, the tree markers need replacing. Ooh. Ooh. This is wonderful. The Girl Scout Council will love it."

(Cheese smilers also gush a lot. Grandpa says you have to take the bad with the good. Sometimes you have to take the good with goop.)

Being helpful is dull. Last year we scraped gypsy moth eggs off the trees and drowned them in gasoline. (I bet the gypsy moths didn't think we were helpful.) The story is that they come out in the spring — zillions of them — and eat the leaves. The eggs look like strips of yellowish-tan fuzz painted on the bark. I thought they were kind of cute. I missed a few, on purpose.

In the winter we dug out fire hydrants each time it snowed. As far as I could tell, it only helped the dogs. Fortunately, it didn't snow a lot.

But this project at Camp Wocka Wocka, I could go for that. If we didn't have to work too hard.

I smiled prettily at Mrs. Wolfe. (You know what I mean: nose up-turned, rosebud mouth, batting my eyelashes, thinking pink thoughts. Queen Karen can turn it on like a faucet. For me it's more like a drip.)

"That's just what I had in mind, Mrs. Wolfe," I said. (Drip drip.)

Mom was wearing her crocodile face again. (She hadn't passed campfires yet in her leader lessons.) The rest of the meeting I followed Mrs. Wolfe around like a baby duckling. It was safer that way.

Mrs. Wolfe quickly figured the project out. School was going to be dismissed for a teachers' convention in early November. "We'll have a long weekend at Wocka Wocka. Plenty of time for work *and* play," she said. Everybody cheered. Except Mom. She snapped her jaws. I waddled closer to Mrs. Wolfe.

After the troop voted yes on the flag, Mrs. Wolfe let us plan our menu for the weekend. The menu was totally scrumptious. First of all, pancakes every day for breakfast — chocolate chip pancakes the first morning, jam pancakes the second morning, fluffernutter pancakes the next (that's marshmallow and peanut butter). We saved the best for last. Bubble-gum pancakes.

Bonnie and I volunteered for the job of going to the shoe store and buying the gum. The ones in the gumball machine are the only kind that work in bubble-gum pancakes. They're so stale they hold their shape.

For lunches it was hot dogs and potato chips, hot dogs and potato chips, hot dogs and potato chips, and hot dogs and potato chips.

If you think that's good, wait until you hear the rest. For dinner: Spaghetti tacos. Egg rolls and bacon. Hamburger heros. And ketchup pizza — with double cheese. No healthy food for four days! I couldn't wait!

15.

Round Louie's

Mom and Mrs. Wolfe decided we should rent a large van for our trip to Wocka Wocka so that all our camping gear and all the girls would fit into one vehicle. "That way if one gets lost, we all get lost," said Mrs. Wolfe, cheerily. I didn't care as long as I didn't have to be lost with Ruth Ellen.

A couple of days before our camping trip Mom and I drove over to Round Louie's Car Corral to reserve our van. A huge wooden cutout of a man lassoing a car with horns stood out in front. He looked like a beach ball wearing a cowboy hat. Probably that was Round Louie.

In the parking lot we saw rows and rows of cars and jeeps and trucks. But no vans. Round Louie must have corraled these at a smashup derby. Most of them looked as if they had been driven blindfolded.

"I don't know, Mom," I cautioned.

"It doesn't have to be beautiful. All we need is something to get us there."

"And back."

"Don't worry, dear. These rental places would go out of business if their cars weren't reliable. We don't want to spend all our Girl Scout money on transportation. We want to spend it on improvements at Wocka Wocka. Isn't that right, dear?" Mom had gotten into the swing of things since I told Mrs. Wolfe that the flag for Wocka Wocka was sort of Mom's idea. Mrs. Wolfe took it from there. My mother's a sucker for compliments.

While we were looking for round things named Louie, Mom went one way and I went the other. I zigzagged between the cars. They were packed together like jellybeans in a jar. I could hardly see where I was going. This parking lot would be the perfect place to lose someone, I thought. Someone short. Heh heh. Someone short like Miss Halibut. Or Ruth Ellen.

I spotted a squatty little shack over in a corner of the lot. When I got closer I realized it was made of spare parts. The walls were tires and hubcaps. The door was a car door. The window was the windshield from a truck. (With wipers. To keep the window clear on rainy days I suppose.) And all around it were rearview mirrors stuck in the ground. (Flowers, maybe?)

In the middle of a patch of rearview mirrors was a gumball machine, which made me think of bubblegum pancakes. I was kicking myself because I hadn't brought any pennies. The bubble gum at car dealerships is almost as good as the gum at shoe stores.

Then I read the sign posted on the machine. This is what it said:

ROUND LOUIE'S ROAD INSURANCE. PUT IN A
QUARTER AND GET 25 PIECES OF INSURANCE
WITH EXTRA ADHESIVE POWER FOR
EMERGENCY REPAIRS. REPAIRS GOOD UNTIL
ROUNDUP TIME.

I scratched my head. They looked like gumballs to me.

I pulled open the door. The hinges squeaked. They needed a grease job. I peeked around a pile of car seats and I was face to face with a man in a ten-gallon hat and a pair of holsters slung on his hips. Over his heart he wore a red reflector. I looked down at his guns. They looked exactly like Jeff's — the ones Grandpa gave him to protect himself from desperadoes, when he went to kindergarten. This guy's were plastic, too.

"Uh, Mr. Round Louie?"

"Howdy, pardner," the man drawled in a heavy cowboy movie accent. "The handle's Tex Mex. What can I do ya for?"

It was Mr. Klunkermeyer! The vacuum-cleaner man! "Hi, Mr. Klunkermeyer!"

Mr. Klunkermeyer quickly put a finger to his lips. "Shhh," he whispered, glancing around behind him.

"Is something wrong, Mr. Klunkermeyer?"

"Round Louie doesn't know my real name. He thinks I'm Tex Mex, the famous Dallas Cowboy. I told him I chased down car rustlers for Wild Bill's Road-E-O out West. Years ago I did live in California and I was a security guard once." Mr. Klunkermeyer hung his head. "But I've never busted a car theft ring. Not one."

Poor Mr. Klunkermeyer. "I guess the cookies didn't help."

"Oh, they made a wonderful mess, but business went downhill so much I had to eat them. I gained six pounds," said Mr. Klunkermeyer.

That made me wonder about Miss Flossy. Maybe her customers gained weight, too. I hoped it helped business at the health spa.

"Hey. Mr. Klunkermeyer—"

"Tex Mex."

"Oh, sorry, Mr. Tex Mex." I winked. "I must have you mixed up with someone else.

"Would you mind not saying anything to my mother about the cookies? She'd make me eat my Girl Scout uniform if I ever mentioned peanut-butter jumbles again."

Mr. Klunkermeyer nodded sympathetically. "My lips are sealed."

"My mom and I are looking for a large van to rent for our camping trip. Do you have any?"

Mr. Klunkermeyer tucked a finger under the brim of his ten-gallon hat. I think he was thinking. Then he twinkled from ear to ear. "Do I have a deal for you! This is better than a van. Very reasonably priced. No operator's license required. It sweeps the sidewalk as you ride. Would you like a low-frills demonstration?"

"Gosh, Mr. Klunker — I mean Mr. Tex Mex — I could use a high-powered vacuum cleaner for fast getaways from the populars and such, but I don't know if I can afford it, since I'm usually having my allowance docked."

"Super-deluxe. Very environmentally protective."

Mr. Klunkermeyer never had a chance to finish. The door creaked just then and Mom came in. She was panting. "Round Louie?"

Mr. Klunkermeyer twirled his toy guns. "Tex Mex is the name. Ask me again and I'll tell ya the same."

After Mr. Klunkermeyer finally had what we wanted straight, we followed him to a second parking lot behind the trees. These were the real heaps. Every time Mom kicked a tire, a fender or a bumper would fall off. Mr. Klunkermeyer would just pick up the fender and press it back on again.

"That man looks strangely familiar to me," said Mom.

I played dumb. It was the least I could do. After all, Mr. Klunkermeyer wasn't mentioning peanut-butter jumbles. "You know used car salesmen, Mom. They all look alike."

First he showed us a camper. It reminded me of a stretched igloo covered with aluminum foil. "Nope. Too small," said Mom.

Then Mr. Klunkermeyer showed us a hearse. It had been pointed with Day-Glo pink, blue, and green racing stripes.

Mom shuddered. "Forget it. It still looks like a funeral car."

At last Mom found what she wanted. A big, yellow school bus. It was cheap, too. "Now, what could be more solid than a school bus?" said Mom, as she kicked a tire. She didn't notice the taillight that fell off.

On the way back to our car Mr. Klunkermeyer let me borrow two quarters and I bought fifty pieces of Round Louie's Road Insurance. This stuff better work, I thought.

16.

Welcome to the Age of En*brighten*ment!

The night before our troop was supposed to leave on the camping trip I had nightmares: the bus started blowing bubbles and came apart halfway to Wocka Wocka. When we tried to stick the pieces together again, I ended up with bubble gum all over my chin.

After that I couldn't go back to sleep. I kept thinking about how much it hurt to scrape the gum off. I called Bonnie on the walkie-talkie. I told her about Round Louie's Car Corral and the gumball insurance.

"I think Roundup Time is when they tow you and your broken-down car home," I said. "I'm worried, Bonnie."

I overslept in the morning because of the nightmares. I was rushing around, packing my duffel bag. Queen Karen opened one eye. "Boy, am I going to love having my room all to myself," she said and shut her eyelid.

"Don't get too used to it or anything, Queenie," I

said. "I'm planning to come back and ruin your life."

"Good-bye, snarf. Have a lousy time."

"Same to you, Your Lowness." Only Queen Karen knows how to start my day.

The troop was meeting at the school parking lot. Dad and Jeff came along with Mom and me to help with the luggage and to say good-bye. Tex Mex was already there. He leaned against the school bus, the keys dangling on the end of a spark plug plugged into his sharpshooter.

Tex Mex whirled his gun and flipped the keys to Mom. "Have a mighty fine trip, ma'am," he said and touched his hat. Tex flashed a wink my way and strode off.

"I've seen that man before," said Dad.

"You know used car dealers," answered Mom. "They all look alike."

Jeff poked me in the ribs. "Wowie! A real cowboy. I wish I could have seen his horse."

"Oh, his horse isn't much. It has a long tail, three small wheels, and trots very close to the ground."

"Horses don't have wheels."

"His does."

The school bus was so roomy we didn't have any trouble fitting ourselves and our gear on. But when we finished, one end of the bus was much higher than the other. "Maybe we have a flat, Jean," said

Mrs. Wolfe, who was clutching a pole to keep from sliding downhill.

Mom called out the window to Dad. "Do we have a flat tire?"

"No," said Dad after a few minutes, "but it's squatting badly. What did this Tex Mex guy rent you?"

The girls scrambled to get off. I took a look. The bus was parked on its rear end like a mule. After we shifted the sleeping bags and the tents and the cooking equipment and the suitcases toward the middle, the bus looked like a bowlegged mule, but at least it stood on all fours.

"All aboard!" shouted Mom.

Bonnie and I sat in the front, as far away as possible from Ruth Ellen and her populars. Bonnie was on one side of the aisle and I was on the other.

Mom started the engine. My teeth gritted, waiting for something to blow. Nothing blew. Not even bubbles. The engine sounded very — well, engine-y. I relaxed. Maybe we'd make it to Wocka Wocka after all.

We were bumping along through town, when Bonnie called on the walkie-talkie. She had to do it hidden under her jacket. We didn't want the other kids to know about them. "Masked Man to Mean Maxine. Come in." I hadn't expected her to call so soon. My walkie-talkie was still in my backpack.

I was standing on the seat reaching for it when Mom made a right turn and drove over a curb. I fell spread-eagled on the other seat on top of Bonnie.

"Unf."

"Sorry, Bonnie," I whispered into the jacket.

"I said come in. Not come over," Bonnie hissed through a sleeve.

"I will. I will. Give me a chance." I climbed over the seats to my side and started to get my pack.

All of a sudden the bus screeched to a halt and I found myself swinging from the overhead rack. This time Mom was stopping for a red light.

Down below there was a landslide. Our equipment had plowed to the front of the bus and the bus was tipping like a seesaw. "Hurry, girls, line up. Like a bucket brigade," Mrs. Wolfe ordered. Everybody quickly lined up and passed things back until the bus was righted.

"Marvelous," said Mrs. Wolfe, flashing her famous cheese smile.

The traffic signal turned green. The cars ahead of us drove away. Our bus roared, then grumbled, then sat absolutely still. Traffic behind us piled up. First one driver leaned on his horn, a second one answered, and another one joined in. Then another, and another.

HONK! HONK! HONK! HONK!

BLEAT! BLEAT!

AROOGAH! AROOGAH!

"Hey, lady, they don't make them any greener," said a policeman beside Mom's window.

Mom was punching buttons and pulling levers as fast as she could. "I'm doing the best I can, officer." (Mom made a face at him when he wasn't looking.)

We sat through more green lights, while the policeman directed traffic around us. In the middle of a red light the bus sort of hopped part way into the intersection. "Whoa!" The policeman dodged. "You can't go now, lady."

"Officer, do you want me to get this wreck out of here or not? I have the feeling this may be our only chance."

The policeman mopped his face. "Okay, lady. Get it OUT of here."

We pulled away. Mom patted the steering wheel. "I think I like this job."

I was fumbling in the overhead rack for the third time when I realized there was a rather stiff breeze up there. My head felt as if it was preparing for liftoff. I raised a hand to check. My head was all there, but my hair definitely was trying to leave. It was streaming past my nose, pointing toward a heating vent near the ceiling.

"Masked Man to Mean Maxine. Over." Bonnie was sounding impatient.

I kept the walkie-talkie inside my pack and talked into the zipper. "Mean Maxine to Masked Man. Over."

"Hi, Max. It's me," Bonnie whispered.

"No kidding."

"Can you hear me? How is everything out there?" Bonnie's voice was sort of muffled and wavy, in time to the bouncing of the bus.

"I can hear you. Everything's fine, except I think I'm going bald."

"Bald? Over."

"Yeah, the hair feels like it's being sucked right off my head."

I saw a tissue fly past. It must have been Fran's. She's always blowing her nose. Woosh! There went part of Mrs. Wolfe's paper. Right out of her lap. It took off so fast she didn't even know what happened. Woosh! Jennifer's Girl Scout beanie flew by. They slammed into the heating vent and fought their way inside. Slurp! Slurp! "I think this is a very hungry school bus, Bonnie. It eats paper and hats and is thinking about taste-testing brown hair. Over."

Bonnie popped her head out from under her coat, then popped back inside. "Max, speaking as your lawyer, you better get down from there. Something funny is going on. Over."

"You're telling me," I said, ducking to avoid a knockout punch from a paper lunch sack. I dropped to my seat.

The bus slowed. We were approaching the turnpike. All the tollbooths except one were closed, which meant that a lot of traffic had to funnel into a single lane.

"You're doing beautifully, Jean," said Mrs. Wolfe. Mom didn't look beautiful. She looked sweaty. The bus was at right angles to the tollbooth.

Mrs. Wolfe stuck her head out the window and waved cars out of the way. One guy wouldn't move, so Mom put the bus in reverse and did a few backward loopy-loops to position it. "Good. One more time," said Mrs. Wolfe. (After a couple of those the guy that wouldn't move couldn't move fast enough.)

At last the bus rolled into the ticket lane. Front first. (Phew.)

Mrs. Wolfe turned to the girls. She swung her arms high. "How about a Girl Scout thank you for the bus driver? HIP HIP HOORAY! HIP HIP HOORAY! HIP HIP HOORAY!" Then she conducted us in a cheer.

> PAH PAH PAH!
> DIDDELEY DIDDELEY RAH!
> PAH PAH PAH!
> DIDDELEY DIDDELEY RAH!
> MRS. GOODE! MRS. GOODE!
> SHE'S NOT BAD!

Even I was cheering. "MRS. GOODE! MRS. GOODE! SHE'S NOT BAD!"

Then we stopped. All of us. There was dead silence.

Puffy clouds of smoke were pouring from under the hood of the bus and streaming into the tollbooth. The attendant was churning his arms like a fan. Smoke began slipping inside the bus window.

Mrs. Wolfe blew her whistle. TWE-E-E-T. TWE-E-E-T. "Now down on the floor, girls. Out the emergency exit in the back. Girls in the rear, open the doors." That was Ruth Ellen and her populars. I hoped they weren't too popular to know what to do. "That's right," said Mrs. Wolfe. (Phew.) "Chop, chop, girls." I hadn't crawled this fast since Jeff was in diapers and he and I raced Arf around the dining room table.

Mrs. Wolfe led us to a grassy area beside the toll plaza. "One. Two. Girls. One. Two. March."

We watched as the smoke continued to pour. "Do you think it will blow up, Mrs. Goode?" Bonnie asked.

"Oh, goody. I hope it does," said Ruth Ellen. (She would.) Even though my mother and her mother are best friends, Mom gave Ruth Ellen her iceberg look. Mom's iceberg look could freeze a popular.

Then the bus rattled and gasped one last cloud of smoke. The air around the tollbooth started to clear.

"Wait till I get my hands on that phony cowboy," said Mom. "He'll wish he'd stuck with wooden horses."

Mom looked mad enough to quit. I couldn't believe it. Here Bonnie and I had worked so hard and Mr. Klunkermeyer was going to do it!

"What'll we do now?" said one of the girls.

Ruth Ellen tittered. "We could call up the Boy Scouts." (She would.)

But that gave me an idea. We could use the walkie-talkie to call for help. I had left the school bus in such a hurry I forgot it. After the smoke finished clearing, I went to climb back inside. I stuck my head in and a strange smell hit me. That wasn't smoke. That was Raspberry-Rhubarb!

I rushed outside and threw open the hood. I should have known. Miles of hose snaked like spaghetti around the engine and the radiator. Attached to the hoses were brush nozzles, fabric nozzles, crevice nozzles, even a beater bar, all tucked in among parts I usually saw when Grandpa worked on his car.

I leaned in closer and found a vacuum cleaner bag. I sniffed the bag. Raspberry-Rhubarb, just as I suspected. Must be Raspberry-Rhubarb didn't sell.

There was an envelope taped to the bag and inside I found this note. "Congratulations!" it said. "You have witnessed the first demonstration of the self-activating, self-educating, self-healing Super-Deluxe Flex-O-Matic Garbage Transporter and Scrubber. The first of its kind. Invented by K. R. Meyer, Esquire. You've heard of the Stone Age. You've heard of the Bronze Age. You've heard of the Machine Age. You've heard of Teen-Age. This is the Clean 'n' Gleam Age. Welcome to the Age of En**brighten**ment!"

K. R. Meyer? What did the R stand for?

"Note: Empty bag when full." The bag appeared to be quite full, so I opened it. Mrs. Wolfe's newspaper, Jennifer's beanie, the lunch bag, Fran's tissue, a little brown hair, they were all there.

"Don't tell me you know how to fix buses, too." It was Mrs. Wolfe behind me.

"I was just looking around. Sometimes I help my grandfather. Uh, here's your newspaper," I said and handed it to her.

"How do you suppose that got in there?"

"Uh, you see this? It's the Garbage Transporter and Scrubber. It transported it—" I traced the hoses—"to here."

"I see. To here."

"Yeah. It's a new feature on school buses these days. It was sucking instead of blowing. But I can fix it. You'd be amazed at what's changed since you were a kid. School buses and insurance. Insurance has changed a lot, too."

"My, you children are growing up in a different world," marveled Mrs. Wolfe. "You're so much smarter than we were."

17.

Tentmates

Fixing the bus was easy. While Mrs. Wolfe was looking the other way, I just yanked out the Garbage Transporter and stashed it in the toll booth. I still had the fifty pieces of bubble gum left for the return trip. At this rate, I'd need them.

Too bad fixing the school bus couldn't count toward a Girl Scout badge, I thought. All I have is the Pets badge, for taking care of Arf and Jeff.

The school bus smelled, but it ran fine all the rest of the way to Camp Wocka Wocka. We had a flag-raising ceremony first thing after we arrived. Fran played the bugle. Fran had never played the bugle before and it sounded like it.

Bonnie and I tied the new flag to the rope and hauled it to the top of the flagpole while everyone saluted. I felt proud of our new flag, even if the bugle did make me think of a moose with a belly-ache.

Until Ruth Ellen noticed the flag was upside

down. "The stars are supposed to be on top," she said.

I looked up. Darn Ruth Ellen Wolfe.

Ruth Ellen pointed to Bonnie and me. "They don't even know which end is up. Ha ha." A couple of the girls laughed: darling Darlene and Lucy. Lucy laughs at everything Ruth Ellen does. She laughs if Ruth Ellen breathes. You'd think Ruth Ellen was funny.

I didn't think Ruth Ellen was funny. I thought Ruth Ellen was rotten. "How would you know?" (I muttered, in case my mother was listening.) "You're upside down yourself, you bat. You hang around in moldy caves and you have dirty toenails where your brains ought to be. That's how upside down you are."

"Have you noticed something, Maxie? You're always talking to yourself."

"Oh yeah?" I *hate* it when Ruth Ellen calls me Maxie. I drilled her with my Mean Maxine stare. "That's so I can talk to someone intelligent, Wolfie."

"Miss Halibut says muttering reflects a bad attitude."

Oooh! One flying scissors kick right to the chops and I'd feel so good.

Bonnie must have read my mind. She poked me. "I don't think I could get you off on temporary insanity. Clobbering her would be too sane. Come on. Help me lower the flag."

Bonnie and I refastened the flag and raised it to the tune of more moose pains. "You know something, Bonnie? My mother has zero taste in best friends' daughters."

"Sub-zero."

Mrs. Wolfe blew her whistle. "Okay, busy-busy, girls. It's fall service project time."

Camp Wocka Wocka should have been named Camp Worka Worka. Mrs. Wolfe went overboard with our service project and we not only had to de-smell all the outhouses, we had to rake and clean every inch of the whole, the *entire*, campground. Mom and Mrs. Wolfe were right behind us, checking.

"We'll enjoy the fruits of our labors later, girls."

I could have used more fruit and less labor. In fact, I was beginning to wish that we had handed over a new flag at a village council meeting, then saluted and beat it, the way my mother wanted to in the first place.

But the worst was yet to come.

Before the evening campfire Mom announced we would be drawing names for tentmates. "And no swapping, girls." She made a point of looking at me. "This is a chance to become better acquainted with someone in the troop you don't know as well."

"Better acquainted?" I sputtered. "Bonnie and I were going to tent together. We had it arranged." What were they trying to do? Ruin the trip?

Mrs. Wolfe handed me a beanie. Inside the beanie were a lot of pieces of folded paper. I rummaged in the pieces of paper. Please. Please, let it be someone I can stand. I picked a name.

RUTH ELLEN WOLFE

I read the paper three times, hoping my eyesight would instantly improve. Each time the letters were the same.

What a disaster. It would take me years of camp to adjust.

I bet anything my mother was behind this. Probably there was a separate beanie for me, and every tiny slip of paper had Ruth Ellen's name on it. Mom really had me fooled back at the tollbooth when she gave Ruth Ellen that iceberg look. I thought she had forgotten about social skills. I thought she was on my side now, instead of the populars'. The next time I walked past her I hissed, "Double-crosser."

"Let's cooperate, dear."

Mrs. Wolfe called for attention. "Now that you've picked your tentmates, and I'm sure everybody's happy—"

(Twelve Girl Scouts groaned.)

"—you may pitch your tents." Mrs. Wolfe scurried about giving us instructions on how to put them up. "Stretch your tents out on the ground. Then you'll know where to position the stakes. No, Linda, you must not use the ropes as a clothesline. Your tent will sag. Remember, girls, whatever you do, in the morning, *don't* touch the canvas. That breaks the air bubbles and the dew or rain will leak through."

Ruth Ellen and I sat and glared at each other, leaving our pup tent untouched.

"Move along, Ruth Ellen," Mrs. Wolfe said. "Or you won't have yours up in time for bed."

Actually, I was hoping we would never get it up.

"Don't look at me," said Ruth Ellen. "This wasn't my idea."

I scowled. "Do you want to hammer or hold the stakes?"

"I don't know how to hammer."

"Figures. Populars only know how to wash their hair."

They also don't know how to hold stakes. On the first smash Ruth Ellen stuck her thumb under the mallet.

She howled loud enough to shatter a few nearby eardrums. Namely, mine. "Help! I need a doctor!"

"Maybe you need an undertaker," I suggested.

Then I got a lecture from my mother on sympathy. I almost missed the sing-along. The tent finally went up, no thanks to Ruth Ellen. Bonnie helped me. At least a lawyer can hold stakes.

I didn't learn many social skills. All Ruth Ellen did was worry about her thumb and where to put her mirror. That was as much as I learned.

Ruth Ellen had gone to sleep. I was squirming on the rocks that poked through my sleeping bag. I think it was because I wasn't used to being so close to a popular. It gave me this wormy feeling. I decided to call Bonnie.

"She even sleeps like she's popular," I said. "I watched her. She closed her eyes — she has this angel smile — and in seconds she was dreaming already. Bonnie, do you think it's a social skill?"

"What?"

"Sleeping with a smile on your face."

"Could be. Ask your mother."

The thought of spending all night watching Ruth Ellen smile was making me depressed, so I signed off. "Good night, Bonnie. I'm glad you don't have social skills."

"Me too. Good night."

I pulled apart the tent flaps and watched the fire for something else to do. It was starting to drizzle. The fire was dying down. Every once in a while a spark would fly and I'd think of a great name to call Ruth Ellen.

Snap! Pop! Ruth Ellen Pickle Lips. Snap! Crackle! Ruth Ellen Petunia. Snap! Fizz! Ruth Ellen Mush Melon.

I turned to Ruth Ellen's beautiful sleep smile. "Hi, Petunia," I said. Ruth Ellen kept on smiling.

"Hi, Petunia. Petunia. Petunia." I said it this way: Pit-tooooooon-YAH! The last syllable was like a karate chop. Hi-iii-YAH!

Dreaming up insults was very relaxing and must

have helped me to fall asleep because the next thing I knew I was waking up and I was drowning in rainwater because Ruth Ellen was standing up inside the pup tent.

(Pup tents are sitting-and-skootching-in-and-out-on-your-knees-or-fanny tents, not standing-up-and-pulling - your - candy - pink - nightgown - over - your - head tents.)

I yawned. "Someone touched the canvas."

Ruth Ellen's hair and wet nightie clung to her like plastic wrap.

"Smile," I said. "Or do you only do that at night?"

"This is not funny." Ruth Ellen stomped her foot. "You are disgusting and awful and —" Ruth Ellen stomped her foot and swung her arms.

That's when the tent fell down.

18.

One Turn Deserves Another

Ruth Ellen Tattletale told Mom I kicked her and punched her when we were trying to get out of the tent. I have to admit I did sneak in a few jabs. Only jabs though, no punches. The rest were accidents.

I wish I *had* punched her. Mom was treating Ruth Ellen as if she was a saint for tenting with me. "What about me?" I yowled. "Look at what I have to put up with."

"Ruth Ellen is a lovely girl," said Mom. "*You* need to learn some consideration."

"But *she* knocked the tent down, not me. What am I supposed to do — politely ask directions to the nearest exit? It was dark in there. I was suffocating." I gasped a few times to make my point.

Ruth Ellen whimpered again. Mom wrapped an arm around her. "There, there. You'll be all right." It was clear who was going to get sympathy and who wasn't. I wasn't. "You should be ashamed of yourself, Maxine. You frightened her."

Me frighten *her?* After she practically buried me alive?

This sort of injustice called for a conference with my lawyer. Bonnie and I met at the pump after breakfast while Bonnie brushed her teeth. "Old Ruth Ellen Mush Melon made it sound as if everything was my fault, and she didn't do a thing."

Bonnie stopped brushing. "One good turn deserves another."

"Is that another one of your precedents?" I asked. Bonnie nodded and continued scrubbing. She scrubs for a long time. "Does that mean one *rotten* turn deserves another?"

Bonnie smiled through the toothpaste foam. I could tell she was saying yes. "Thanks, Bonnie. That's the nicest thing anybody has said to me all day. I'm going to find the perfect turn for Ruth Ellen. Something awful."

But it wasn't enough to be awful. It had to get her into trouble, the same way she had gotten me into trouble — for something I didn't do. Then we would be even.

I thought about it all morning while we did more worka worka on our service project. Today's job was to clear three trails that went around the lake and repaint the trail markers.

Mom came up with a system for everyone to stay in touch even though we couldn't see each other.

One patrol yelled the color of its trail, then when the other two patrols heard it, they yelled their color. Whoever was last yelled first on the next round.

We had these long chains of calls:
"Red!"
  "Blue!"
    "Yellow!"
    "Yellow!"
      "Red!"
        "Blue!"
        "Blue!"
          "Yellow!"
            "Red!"
            "Red!"
              "Yellow!"
                "Blue!"
                "Blue!"
                  "Yellow!"

Then *somebody* would scream "Green!!" (Heh heh) and goof up the whole works.

Once our patrol didn't answer, just to see what would happen. A few minutes later we could hear Mom crashing through the trees. "Red? Where are you, Red?" She had almost caught up with us.

We screeched. "Red!!!"

"Oh, hi, Mom."

"It's — about — time," she puffed.

"Time? Oh that. Sorry. We forgot which color we were."

We did that twice. Once more and Mom would have knocked a few beanies together.

Lunch rolled around and I was still trying to come up with the Perfect Turn to do to Ruth Ellen. I had some ideas, but they weren't perfect because they weren't rotten enough. This one had to be perfectly rotten.

I was cleaning paint off my hands — you knew which trail we had worked on by our skin color; I was red to my wrists, both of them — when Mom sidled up to me. She pretended to be concentrating on something over my head. "I want you to apologize to Ruth Ellen," she whispered.

"I can't say I'm sorry, because I don't feel sorry."

"You owe her an apology," Mom insisted.

"You're just worried about what Mrs. Wolfe will say." Mom blushed. Then, as I worked on my fingers, the Perfect Turn came to me. I knew how I was going to make Ruth Ellen pay. I pouted (so that I wouldn't look happy). "Ruth Ellen would never believe me anyway."

"You can't be sure until you try," Mom said, hoping.

I made it look as if I was thinking about it. "Okay, I'll try. But don't blame me if it doesn't work."

"That's all I ask. That you try." Mom patted me on the back. "Thank you, Maxine. I know you can handle it."

"I can handle it," I said, relishing the thought.

I called Bonnie over. She was still munching her hot dog. "Bonnie, I have to apologize to Ruth Ellen for this morning. But she won't come near me with a ten-foot comb. Lawyers represent people, right?"

Ketchup oozed out of the bottom end of Bonnie's roll. "Yeah."

"I want you to represent me. Go tell her I want to talk to her, so I can say I'm sorry."

Bonnie studied my head as though I'd lost something, like a few marbles. "What about one rotten turn deserves another?"

"Just do it. I'll explain later."

"Okay," Bonnie said, puzzled.

While Bonnie was talking to Ruth Ellen for me I found a balloon in my duffel bag. I carry a lot of useful items in my duffel bag: Slime, Krazy Glue, and balloons for water bombs. I used to carry rotten bananas until my mother made me stop because of the fruit flies.

Bonnie returned. "Forget it. Mush Melon doesn't want your apology."

"Great!"

"Great?"

I explained my plan to Bonnie. Bonnie loved it. "Count on me, Max."

Then I ran to tell my mother what Ruth Ellen had said. "She won't even talk to me. How can I apologize if she won't talk to me?" I slumped on the ground. "I give up."

"No, don't give up. Let me speak to her," said Mom.

Oh boy. Oh boy. Things were going *perfectly*.

After Mom left I hurried to my place on a log near the tents. Bonnie was waiting for me, hidden behind a tree where Ruth Ellen wouldn't be able to see her, but where Bonnie could see Ruth Ellen and me.

A while later I heard darling Darlene and Lucy, giggling. "There she is." Ruth Ellen must have sent them to find me. Then Ruth Ellen herself showed up.

"What do you want, gruesome?" she said. "Your mother said you wanted to talk to me, gruesome."

I spoke so sweetly in return that if I had been listening to myself I would have made myself sick. "I just wanted to tell you how really, really, really and truly, truly sorry I am about knocking the tent down on you, and kicking you and punching you — by the way, I also jabbed you — and for jabbing you this morning."

"Huh?"

"It was a terrible, terrible thing for one Girl Scout to do to another. Especially to such a likable and popular person such as you. My mother has made me see that. I want you to know I will carry the sorrow of that wrong I did to you in my heart until the day I croak." At that point I laid my hands over my heart.

Lucy giggled.

"I want to promise you my never-ending loyalty and friendship. And as proof of my never-ending loyalty and friendship I want to give you the Girl Scout handshake. Will you ever forgive me?" I faked a few tears.

"You don't have to cry about it," said Ruth Ellen.

"Yes, I do. My mother won't let me back in the family until we do this." My voice had grown hoarse and quavery.

Ruth Ellen laughed. "Did you take cuckoo pills or something?"

She was going to make me sweat this one out, I could see that. "Please?"

"Can't make me."

"My mother will tell your mother," I snarled.

"Oh, all right. But this is dumb." Ruth Ellen raised her right hand. I raised my right hand, and . . .

Ker-fwoosh! Splat! As soon as we raised our hands for the Girl Scout handshake — that was Bonnie's and my signal — Bonnie pelted me with a paint-filled balloon. Ruth Ellen never knew what hit me. Blue paint oozed down my ear, down my neck, onto my arm. From there it puddled onto my basketball hightops.

Ruth Ellen gasped. Lucy giggled.

I shrieked bloody murder. And raced for my mother. "She threw paint at me. Ruth Ellen threw paint at me. I was trying to apologize and she threw paint at me. Look at me. I'm covered with paint. I'll be blue for the rest of my life. I'll never be happy again. I'm ruined."

Mom couldn't believe her eyes. Neither could Ruth Ellen. "But — but — I didn't throw any paint. I raised my hand — and —"

"We were raising our hands for a Girl Scout handshake and she popped me with it. What a dirty trick."

Mom watched the dripping paint. "Ruth Ellen, dear," said Mom, "that's no way to settle a disagreement. I'm surprised at you."

"But I didn't —"

"I'm going to have to tell your mother about this. I think you owe Maxine an apology." Mom quickly found something to wipe up the paint. "Poor, poor Maxine," she clucked. "What a terrible thing to have happen."

19.

Anchors Aweigh

That afternoon we were playing Frisbee — my team was destroying Ruth Ellen's team — when the Frisbee went for a swim. We could see it floating about halfway across the lake. "Oh dear. That ends our afternoon recreation," said Mrs. Wolfe.

"Of course not," said Mom. "There's a rowboat, isn't there? I'll take the boat out and get it." Mom's campfires weren't going too well. I think she wanted to show Mrs. Wolfe she could do something.

(At Mom's rowing classes they put a boat in the "Y" swimming pool. Once she broke an oar on the bottom because she forgot to glide at the kiddie end, but they passed her anyway since the water in Lake Wocka Wocka is deeper.)

Mom put on an orange life preserver, climbed into the boat, and began pulling on the oars. Mom rowed the way I walk — pigeon-toed. First to one side, then the other, but basically forward.

She was close enough to reach the Frisbee, but every time she touched it, it slipped away. Mrs.

Wolfe hollered, "You need a crew. Come back and bring a couple of the girls to help you."

Bonnie and I volunteered. Mom picked us up and then all three of us went after the Frisbee. But the same thing happened. The boat drifted one way and the Frisbee the other.

"Drop the anchor!" Mrs. Wolfe shouted.

"Here it is," said Bonnie, tugging on a rope in the bottom of the boat. At the end of the rope was a flat concrete disk. It was so heavy Bonnie and I could barely grunt as we pushed it over the side.

Ka-Blam! The anchor made a huge splash, filling the rowboat with water. When we came up for air, we had to quick bail it out.

"Where did the Frisbee go?" said Mom, water pouring down her face.

"It's still here. Wipe your sunglasses off."

Mom wiped her glasses. "Oh, good. For a minute I thought we'd lost it. I'm going to move to the front and reach for the Frisbee from there. You two sit in the back and keep the weight balanced. Maybe we'll have better luck that way."

Bonnie and I squeezed past Mom in the middle while Mom crawled to the front. She leaned way out over the point. "Hand me an oar," she said, her arm behind her.

I put the oar in her hand. "What are you going to do now?"

Mom positioned the oar in the water beside the

Frisbee and began guiding it toward the boat. "I'm going to pull it in with the oar. Easy now," she told herself. "Easy."

The Frisbee dived and popped out of the water on the wrong side of the oar.

"Pesky little rascal," said Bonnie.

Mom scowled. "Try, try again," she muttered.

"Tsk. Tsk. Muttering reflects a bad attitude."

Mom gave me one of her iceberg looks.

I smiled. "I learned that from Miss Halibut."

"At least you've learned *something* in sixth grade."

Mom positioned the oar again and began guiding the Frisbee ahead of it. This time the oar was moving too fast. A crest of water pushed the Frisbee aside.

"Snicklefritz!" shouted Mom. (Mom doesn't like swearing so she makes up fake swear words. She also says Blastford! But she only uses that one when she's *extremely* mad.)

"Blastford!"

Uh-oh.

"Maybe we should forget it, Mom. Who needs a Frisbee? We can toss rocks. Or tree stumps."

Just then there was another enormous splash. My T-shirt was sopping wet all over again. Bonnie's ponytail was streaming water down her life preserver.

"Too bad we forgot noseplugs," I said.

"And oxygen tanks," said Bonnie.

I looked out over the water. "Hi, Mom. Having a nice time? I like your swim cap. Is that the new style? You ought to remember that one for the Easter parade." Mom was bobbing along in her orange life preserver. Perched on her head was the Frisbee.

Mom spat a long funnel of water. "Hand me the oar."

There are certain times when even I know it is better to follow directions. I handed her an oar and pulled her to the boat.

Bonnie plucked the Frisbee off Mom's head. "Mission accomplished."

Mom threw a leg over the side and hurled herself in. She was shivering. She was also glowering.

"Would you like us to row, Mom?"

"No, thank you," she barked. "The rowing will warm me up."

When Mom's mad, she's fast. She was so mad I figured she ought to set a world record getting to shore. But instead of racing over the water, we crept — one slow inch at a time. Mom panted and strained. She was warming herself up all right. She was red hot. After a while I was worried about reaching land by nightfall. Bonnie and I looked at each other and shrugged. This was no time to ask questions.

FINALLY we made it back. Mom staggered out of the boat and collapsed on the ground.

Patty Ryan and several of the other girls helped haul the boat out of the water. "Hey, what's this?" said Patty. She pointed to a rope hanging from the end of the boat. The rope seemed to be caught on something.

"Maybe it's an octopus!" said Fran.

"I hope it's a mermaid."

Together we pulled on the rope. This was like a tug-of-war. Us against the lake. Up it came, slowly, slowly. Whatever it was was covered with weeds. I hoped it was buried treasure: the treasure of Wocka Wocka.

"It's a dumb old tire," said Ruth Ellen.

"It's the anchor," said Mrs. Wolfe. She turned to Mom. "Jean, it's the anchor. You must have had a terrible time rowing with the anchor still out. Why didn't you bring it into the boat first?"

I guess they didn't have anchors at the "Y". Anyway that was my first rowing lesson: you have to pull up the anchor if you want to go anywhere in a boat. If you want to go anywhere *fast*, I mean.

That night Mom's campfire died before we finished the second Girl Scout song and she couldn't start it up again. We had to use our flashlights. We all sat in a circle, pointing them toward the center where the fire had been, and told ghost stories. One by one we turned them off to make it seem like embers dying. Mom thought it was too artificial. You could tell she felt sort of like a flop.

"Everybody feels like a flop sometimes, Mom. Look at me."

Mom examined my blue ear. "You're right, Maxine. Absolutely right."

20.

Capture the Flag

In the morning I ran into Mom on my way to breakfast duty. I did a double-take. She looked like the
million-year-old woman. The only thing you can do
when your mother has suddenly turned into a fossil
is to be cheerful. "Hi, Mummy," I said. "Whoops. I
mean Mom. Having a rousing good time at Girl
Scout camp, I hope."

Mom's eyes rolled. I think they were saying How-
can-I-possibly-be-having-a-good-time-when-I'm-so-
miserable? Then I noticed that not much else was
moving. Her eyes and her feet were the only moving
parts.

"Your arms and neck seem very rigid this morning. May I help you bend them?"

"NO!! DON'T TOUCH!!" Those probably
were Mom's first words of the day. "If you had slept
on the cold ground beside a cold campfire after you
had rowed an anchor halfway across Lake Wocka
Wocka, you'd be stiff as a board, too."

Mom tried to give me an iceberg look, but her eyebrows weren't cooperating. She looked frozen instead of angry. It's hard to look angry when your eyes and feet are the only moving parts; looking frozen is easier.

Then in a flash it hit me! This might do it. This could be the thing that makes Mom decide to quit Girl Scouts! "Gee, Mom, if I'd known this was going to happen I never would have suggested that game of Frisbee."

I skipped off to breakfast duty. "Tra la la. La la."

While we were eating there was more good news: our Camp Wocka Wocka service projects were done. I yelled as loud as I could. "Ya-aaay!"

"Since this is our last day, we're going to play a hiking game called Capture the Flag," said Mrs. Wolfe.

"Ya-aaay!"

"And since we don't have a flag, other than the new one we're donating to Wocka Wocka — we don't want to use that one, do we? — Mrs. Goode has agreed to be our flag. Three cheers for the flag!"

"HIP HIP HOORAY! HIP HIP HOORAY! HIP HIP HOORAY!"

"This is an excellent opportunity to use our map-reading skills, girls. While Mrs. Goode is finding that little X on your maps — X is the spot where the flag is supposed to be — we can be studying our maps and dividing into teams. The first team to capture the flag" — Mrs. Wolfe giggled — "and bring her back to camp, wins."

Mom looked like a starched shirt walking into the woods. While the troop waited to give her a head start, Bonnie motioned for me to meet her behind the tents.

"Be sure to bring your walkie-talkie on the hike," said Bonnie.

"Why?"

"I didn't want to have to mention this, but before we left for camp I ate dinner with my dad at Mr. Lee's restaurant. There was an extra fortune taped to my Girl Scout cookie. I told my dad, 'This one's for Maxine.'" Bonnie grabbed me by the poncho. "This is our last day here. It has to happen today."

"*What* has to happen today?"

"It said, 'Maintain close ties with family. Bad breaks ahead.'"

"How do you know that fortune wasn't meant for you?"

Bonnie shook her head. There was no doubt in her mind.

I examined each of my arms and legs. "I wonder which one."

"It didn't say."

"Did it say anything else?"

" 'Old wounds heal.' "

"Wounds? Yipes!" And the day had gotten off to such a good start. Rats.

On the hike I was feeling super jittery. Every time a twig snapped I was scared it was me and I watched my legs so much, instead of where I was going, that a couple of times I made a wrong turn.

Then I fell. Bonnie and the others had stopped to read the map. I had gone up a slope to look ahead to the next ridge, and I stepped in a hole.

I looked down at my leg. This is it, I thought, as I hit the ground. I was waiting for terrible pain to overcome me. I'll probably pass out, I thought. I held my breath, waiting.

I was getting dizzy from holding my breath so long, so I took another breath.

Maybe this isn't it, I thought after a while. Maybe this is a pre-test. Like the spelling pre-tests Miss Halibut gives to tell you whether or not you need to cram for the Friday test.

Slowly I got up and dusted myself off. Each limb was still there, in the right place. What do you know? I guess this meant I'd pass the final.

My team had left already. I looked over my map and decided to take a shortcut to catch up with them. I continued up over the slope and down the other side, congratulating myself on passing the pre-test, when what should I see but *my mother* lying beside a small stream like a washed-up trout. I tiptoed over.

"Wonderful," Mom said from the ground. "I didn't expect anyone to find me so soon."

"What are you doing here? You're not supposed to be here. There isn't any stream here." I thought about that for a moment. "There *is* a stream here." I pointed to the one beside her. "But no stream *here*." I pointed to the X on the map.

"I know all that. I was taking a shortcut and I slipped on the rocks." Mom lifted her ankle about a half inch. It was swollen and purplish. "I can't walk on it."

Mom was down to one moving part. Her eyes. This must be the bad break my Girl Scout fortune cookie talked about. It was *Mom's* leg that was going to be broken.

"I tried yelling, but it hurt my neck and shoulders," said Mom. "I knew when you all met at the X and I wasn't there, you would go looking for me. I wasn't worried. Now that you've found me we can get on with the business of transporting me back to camp."

Then I had some of the meanest thoughts I've ever had. "How am I going to get you back? I can't carry you alone."

"You're alone? Well, use that walkie-talkie gizmo you have. Call Bonnie, she'll tell the others, and they'll be here in no time."

"What walkie-talkie gizmo?"

"Maxine, I know you have it here at camp. I've

seen you and Bonnie whispering up your sleeves. Where is it?"

"It might be in my tent."

Just then a voice from inside my poncho said, "Masked Man to Mean Maxine. We've lost contact. Come in, Mean Maxine." I had a severe coughing fit.

Mom glared so hard I thought she would bore holes through my skull.

"I said it *might* be in my tent. I didn't say definitely it was."

"Maxine B. Goode!"

Mom wasn't just repeating my name. That was an order. But when you studied the situation carefully you had to admit she couldn't order pizza, let alone give orders to me. She had one moving part left. Well, that and her mouth. And I was her only means out of the woods. That ought to be worth something, I thought wickedly.

I removed my baseball cap and fingered the Mean Maxine buttons. "How much?"

"What do you mean, how much?"

"It's a cold, heartless world out there, Mom. These days kids would sell their own mothers for a few lousy bucks. I'm a soft touch, though. I'm not going to try to push a hard bargain or anything."

"In other words, you're blackmailing me." Mom was calm until that point, then she flew into a rage.

"Young lady, you wait until we get home. I will do your rear end such a favor — AAAGH!" She grabbed her neck, then her arm, and sank to the ground.

"All right," she moaned quietly, "what do you want?"

"I want to quit Girl Scouts."

"No. Ruth Ellen is no reason to quit Girl Scouts."

"She's not a reason to *stay* in Girl Scouts either."

"My answer is no."

"Okay, have it your way." I sat on the ground beside her. Mom was very still. I folded my legs and rested my chin on my hand. "Think of it this way, Mom. Some people never have social skills. Just like some people never have a good hook shot." I could see her weakening. "Would you really want me to be the kind of person who would go around flinging paint at people's ears?"

Mom raised a frozen eyebrow. "I don't know that you aren't that kind of person."

Finally Mom said, "I like the fact that you and I have something we do together without Karen and Jeff — except for taking Jeff to the *Ling*. That couldn't be helped — but if you don't want to continue with Girl Scouts, it's up to you."

"You do? It is?"

"Yes to both questions. Now will you please call Bonnie?"

"Wait. Let's not be so hasty. If I quit, will you quit?"

"No." Mom gave a stiff sniff. "I'm doing something. I'm learning new skills. It makes me feel like a new person." She looked out at her arms. "Well, almost a new person. Now are you calling Bonnie?"

That was almost too easy. For a minute the thought of Mom being in Girl Scouts without me made me feel funny, as if I'd miss her. Yipes! *Miss* her? What was I saying? Besides, I couldn't waste a good opportunity. There were other things I wanted, maybe more than quitting Girl Scouts. (I'm meaner than even I thought.)

"Not yet," I answered. "I also want my old room back. In yellow. I'm sick of Karen's perfume and of not being able to do what I want to do in my own room."

"I see," murmured Mom. She seemed to consider it. "Okay, but only if you do one other thing for me."

"Tell me what it is first."

"You get rid of your Mean Maxine shirts and buttons and stickers and I'll see you have your old room back."

"No way."

"I have a lot of influence with your father. I think I could convince him the basement is better. Quieter."

I hesitated. "Do I have to throw the Mean Maxine stuff out—or can I keep it and not wear it in public? I spent three years' allowance on the stuff. You wouldn't want me to waste money."

"In your room. That's the only place."

"How about anywhere in our house?"

Mom sighed. "I was hoping I'd never have to see it again. Okay. But not when we have company."

"Is Grandpa considered company?"

Mom sighed again. "No."

"Then it's a deal."

"Finally. Now please call."

"We have to shake."

"Do we have to?" said Mom.

I forgot about Mom's arms. "We could touch hands and not shake. That'll be as good."

"Fine. We'll touch."

We touched hands and I was very careful not to shake.

21.

Bad Breaks Ahead

Bonnie nudged me before we set out with Mom on the Red trail to camp. "What did I tell you? 'Bad breaks ahead.' I wonder if your mother would like a lawyer to sue the Girl Scout Council."

"What would she sue the Girl Scout Council for?"

"For slippery rocks. Reckless endangerment. I'll come up with something." Bonnie fell into one of her trances, thinking about it.

"Hi-yo Silver, snap out of it. Anyway, you said it was supposed to be *my* fortune."

Bonnie shrugged. "Girl Scout fortune cookies aren't as exact as Chinese fortune cookies."

By then all the girls knew we had the walkie-talkies and they begged to try them. Ruth Ellen Mush Melon finagled it so she could go first. She marched ahead of us, singsonging into the walkie-talkie. "Star Commander to troop. Star Commander to troop. Watch out for tree roots. Just saw a squirrel. One Twinkie wrapper. Over." (Some people are as dumb on CB as they are in person.)

Meanwhile, we got Mom out of the woods using a Girl Scout carry. Boy, was I sorry I had turned down the scale. Mom should have stuck to her diet.

Mrs. Wolfe didn't think Mom's foot was broken. "A nasty sprain, Jean. That's what you have," she said, as she wrapped one of those long stretchy bandages around it. "Just stay off your feet for a few days."

"I guess you'll have to drive the school bus tomorrow," said Mom.

Mrs. Wolfe flashed her cheese smile. "A Girl Scout helps wherever she is needed."

We sat Mom on a log with her foot propped on a knapsack, but after a while she was uncomfortable. "You could sit in the bus, Mom," I suggested. (I was trying to be a teeny bit nice to make up for those mean thoughts I had out in the woods.)

"Splendid idea," said Mrs. Wolfe. So we did our Girl Scout carry again and brought Mom to the bus and set her up on a front seat.

"This is much better," said Mom. She was leaning against the side of the bus with her foot out in front of her on the seat cushion.

"Call us if you need anything," said Mrs. Wolfe.

"Wait a minute. How?"

"Out the window."

"My throat." Mom couldn't quite clutch her throat because of her arms, but she got her point across.

"You could use a walkie-talkie," Bonnie offered.

"Splendid again," said Mrs. Wolfe. "See, girls. There's always a way."

One walkie-talkie stayed with Mom and one went with us. Whenever Mom wanted something, or was feeling lonely, she'd call up. "Yellow Bus to Campfire. I'd like to hear that song again. Over." And we would sing "Sipping Cider Through a Straw" or "There Was an Old Woman Who Swallowed a Fly" again.

Later on, Mom told us ghost stories over the walkie-talkie. Is it ever *creepy* to be sitting there in the woods, in the dark, listening to this voice coming from out of nowhere, telling you about a horseman looking for his head. Every time the campfire popped I thought it was his head popping off.

We were getting ready for bed when Mom called. Maybe she was spooked, too. "Yellow Bus to Campfire. Can we arrange another Girl Scout carry? It's too quiet on the bus."

"Campfire to Yellow Bus. It's dangerous in the dark, Jean. Someone might fall." (Mrs. Wolfe shouted into the walkie-talkie. She never could get it straight that it was a walkie-talkie, not a walkie-shoutie.)

"You could drive the bus over here," I said.

Mrs. Wolfe shouted again. "Did you hear that, Jean? I'll drive the bus closer to the tents. How's that? Over."

"Great."

Mrs. Wolfe took a flashlight and headed for the bus. A few minutes later she returned for the keys. "'Be prepared,' I always say." She laughed. In a short while we could hear the rumble of the bus. Mom must have left the walkie-talkie turned on because we could hear them.

"What do I do next, Jean?"

"You pull that one over there. No, not that one. Those are the windshield wipers."

"Ooo!"

"No, no. It's the one that looks like a golf club. Yes, that's it," said Mom. "Pull it." A pause. "Try putting it back on."

At last the bus was moving. We could see the headlights. One pointed toward the tops of the trees, and the other one pointed straight ahead. It was good to know the bus had headlights at least. Then the bus was rolling in our direction, the windshield wipers beating like drums. It seemed to be coming awfully fast.

Then we heard, "The brakes! Put on the brakes!" That was Mom.

"Where are they?"

"Yellow Bus to Campfire! Yellow Bus to Campfire! We're coming through. Run for your lives!"

Mrs. Wolfe's whistle was blowing. **SCREE!!**

We didn't waste any time. Every girl was out of the path of the bus in seconds.

Ruth Ellen jumped in the lake. I wish I'd had time to enjoy it.

The bus mowed down an empty pup tent, just missed the campfire, then aimed dead ahead for a tree. I covered my eyes. Poor Mom. Poor Mrs. Wolfe. I wondered if Mom would have *any* working parts left.

I kept waiting for the explosion. But there wasn't one. I opened my eyes. The bus had stopped *inches* from the tree.

Mrs. Wolfe was so shaky afterward she couldn't walk any better than Mom could. We had to use Girl Scout carries on both of them. We moved them to the campfire. Mrs. Wolfe spoke finally. "So that's where the brake is."

Mom couldn't answer. She wasn't talking yet.

"Brake handles really ought to be in a more convenient location, wouldn't you say, Jean?"

I had a hard time falling asleep that night. I thought about going home tomorrow. I thought a lot about the bus. I thought even more about Mrs. Wolfe driving the bus. Maybe Mom wasn't good at campfires, but at least she could drive, when her ankles weren't sprained. And she told good ghost stories.

"Mean Maxine to Masked Man."

Bonnie yawned into her walkie-talkie. "Yeah?"

"How did they spell it on my fortune?"

"Spell what?"

"Was it b-r-e-a-k-s? Or was it b-r-a-k-e-s?"

"Zzzzzzzzzzzzz."

Either way it wasn't good.

22.

Goode Goode

We made it home from Camp Wocka Wocka. Even
with Mrs. Wolfe driving. I almost didn't believe
it. I pinched myself nine times. The only thing
that happened was we got lost again in the parking
lot at Round Louie's. But we finally found the
shack made of spare parts and inside was a squarish,
baldheaded man wearing a name tag that said
Louie.

"Are you Round Louie?"

"No, that's my brother. I'm Square Louie with
the Square Deal. What can I do for you?"

"We're here to return the school bus we rented.
Where's Mr. Klunk — I mean, where's Mr. Tex
Mex?" I asked.

Mr. Square Louie squinted at me and barked,
"He's on vacation — permanently." Then Mr.
Square Louie changed to all politeness and smiles.
"Eh, you didn't happen to find anything strange in
your rental vehicle, did you?"

"Oh no," said Mrs. Wolfe. "We did have one minor mishap —"

"And one near miss — a tree."

Mrs. Wolfe put her hand over my mouth. "The Garbage Transporter was sucking instead of blowing. But one of our girls fixed it." Mrs. Wolfe winked at me. "We're a very resourceful bunch, we Girl Scouts."

Square Louie gave Mrs. Wolfe a puzzled look. "Garbage Transporter? Right. Well, nice to do business with you."

"How about some Girl Scout cookies, Mr. Square Louie?"

Mrs. Wolfe clapped her hand over my mouth again. "We're all out. Sorry."

Basically, life was the same after Camp Wocka Wocka. Arf and Jeff and Dad were glad to see me. Queen Karen wasn't. Neither was Miss Halibut. But you knew that.

Karen had plastered pictures of rock stars on the door while I was gone. She and her slave were drooling over which one they liked best.

"I like William Wonder of the Fruitcakes. His eyes are so-o gorgeous."

"My favorite is Oliver. He's got such crazy muscles."

"Mean Maxine has more muscle than that thing."

Queen Karen made her famous good-grief face. Then I noticed her hair. She looked as if she had mangled it in a food processor. "Hey, that's some fantastic hairdo," I said. "You've been hard at work beautifying yourself while I was away."

"Like it? It's a home perm."

"Oliver is going to fall all over you. That is, if he likes strangled spaghetti."

Karen slammed the door in my face. Things were back to normal. "I missed you, Karen," I shouted.

It will be nice to have my own door back, I thought, as I studied those creepy guys Karen had pasted up. Maybe I'd like her again, even if she was a popular.

On Monday I was in trouble right away with Miss Halibut. She found a note I had passed to Bonnie on the floor.

> Meet me in the girls' lavatory after social
> studies. I have important, top-secret
> information.
> P.S. Don't let Old Fish Face see this.

Miss Halibut called my mother to school for a conference.

"Mrs. Goode, you've read this note. I find this note shocking and outrageous. Wouldn't you agree?"

Mom hesitated. "Well—"

"I've never in my life had a student who was capable of such shocking and outrageous behavior. Have you ever in your life seen a child capable of such shocking and outrageous behavior?"

(The numbers on my counter were clicking away. Those were the forty-third, forty-fourth, and forty-fifth times I had been called outrageous since I had been in Miss Halibut's class and the fourteenth, fifteeenth, and sixteenth times for shocking. You have to do *something* to amuse yourself.)

"Furthermore, I find it distasteful to have a child come to school with a blue ear and red hands. It distracts the other children."

Mom winced. "Miss Halibut, I agree Maxine's behavior was outrageous, but hardly shocking. Shock implies surprise, and you and I both know there is nothing surprising about this note. Maxine and I will have another one of our talks, if you wish." Mom sounded tired.

"I wish."

"Good-bye, Miss Halibut."

We walked slowly to the car. Mom was still limping. "I hope what you had to tell Bonnie was important enough not to wait till after school."

I hung my head. "Does this mean I don't get my room back?"

We drove to the shopping center to pick up some groceries on the way home. "No. A bargain is a bargain. Besides, I talked to your father yesterday. Before *this* happened. He says it will be a while."

"It will? He'll do it?" I was so excited all my fuses were blowing.

"We'll come up with some other punishment for that note."

"How about no cartoons?"

"How about no TV for the rest of childhood?" I groaned.

"In the meantime, I expect you to do something about those Mean Maxine shirts. Or else the deal is off."

"I will. Right away. Today. I'll go to Abe's Labels while you get the groceries." Abe's Labels was in the same shopping center. "I'll order a new shirt. Okay? You'll like this one, Mom. I promise."

Mom looked at me as if she didn't believe it. "Don't take too long." As I hopped out of the car I heard her say, "Maxine, you don't know how to get into a little trouble. You only know how to get into big trouble. Do me a favor. The next time you pass notes, don't mention Old Fish Face."

"Sure, Mom."

I raced to Abe's Labels. Usually when you open the door, the chimes play the theme from "Monsters of the Jabber Rocky." But this time they played "Row, Row Your Boat." "Mr. Label," I called. "Your best customer is here."

A man dressed in a white fishing hat, a stripy

T-shirt, and a black eyepatch parted the curtains
to the back room. Around his neck he wore a gold
necklace that reminded me of vacuum cleaner hose.
It wasn't Mr. Abe Label.

He stepped to the counter. "How are you, sugar?
Why, I do declare, it's Miss Mean Maxine. How
are you Miss Mean?"

"Mr. Klunk—! I mean, Mr. Tex—!" I bent
close and whispered. "Who are you now?"

Mr. Klunkermeyer talked from behind his hand.
"Mr. Able Label, recently of Atlantic City, Miami,
and Singapore. Spouse of Mabel Label and long
lost brother-in-law of Abe Label. We were recently
reunited after a twenty-year cruise."

"But Mr. Klunkermeyer, you wouldn't have the
same name if Abe is your brother-in-law."

"Shh. He wants to keep the business in the
family." Mr. Klunkermeyer straightened his eyepatch. "What can I do for you, Miss Mean?"

"Are you positive you know how to do this?"

"The name is Able Label."

"You won't slip any nozzles or vacuum cleaner
bags into my shirts?"

"Me?"

"Okay, Mr. Klunkermeyer, I want a reversible
T-shirt. On credit. Ten cents down and five cents a
week until I pay it off. The other Mr. Label lets
me have credit. Because of my allowance problems.

Sometimes my allowance is — uh — interrupted."

"Certainly. I understand."

When Mom and I got home I called Bonnie on the walkie-talkie to ask for a personal consultation. We met by the bushes.

"I'm sorry she found the note, Max. It fell out of my notebook. Honest."

"You're my lawyer. You're supposed to defend me."

"What could I do?"

"You could have said you wrote it. You would have gotten off easy."

"I didn't think of that. What did she do to you?"

"She's making me do a fifteen-page report on halibut and its importance to the fishing industry."

"Ugh. Sorry, Max. By the way, what were you going to tell me in the lavatory?"

"My mom says I can quit Girl Scouts."

"Great!"

"Well, I'm not sure." I thought about what Mom had said about its being the one place we could do things together, without Jeff and Karen. I thought about the *Ling*, all those Girl Scout cookies, and the camping trip. It couldn't have been much fun for her. I had to hand it to Mom. She stuck it out. Mom was tough. Not Mean Maxine tough, but tough. Only a *really* rotten kid would desert a mother like that.

"But, Max, it worked!"

"No, it didn't. My mother isn't quitting. She likes it. But I don't have to stay in."

"You mean you don't *want* to quit if your mother doesn't quit?"

"If I left, who would help her deliver Girl Scout cookies?"

Bonnie paused for a moment. "Ruth Ellen Wolfe."

"Right. I couldn't let that happen. Then my mother would never get off my back about the populars. I couldn't handle all that pressure."

"Gee, I guess you're right."

"What are you going to do, Bonnie? Quit?"

"Are you kidding? I'm your lawyer. How can I defend you from the populars if I quit?"

What a friend. I mean, who else but a friend would stick out Girl Scouts?

Come to think of it, what a mom. Who else but your mother would stick out Girl Scouts for you?

That night I showed Mom my new T-shirt. On the front it said, "GOODE GOODE." (As in goody-goody.) On the back it said, "MAXINE GOODE! MAXINE GOODE! SHE'S NOT BAAD!" (Mr. Klunkermeyer can't spell.)

"That *is* an improvement," said Mom. She gave me a big hug. "Very nice, Maxine. Now that you've lived up to your part of the bargain I'll go talk to your father."

"But—but you said you had talked to him already."

Mom gave me a Mrs. Wolfe cheese smile. "I've lived with you too long, Maxine, not to know your tricks." She tweaked my cheek. "Good night, dear."

Mom doesn't know *all* my tricks. One thing Mom doesn't know is that on the inside my shirt says, "MEAN MAXINE" in Glow-in-the-Dark letters. With a picture of a sword. Chopping through a huge mush melon.